What people are saying about Jenny Gardiner's books:

Red Hot Romeo

"Awesome". So enjoyed the romantic chemistry between the two characters. Read it non stop into the wee hours. Highly recommend this book
-- Mrs. K

Blue-Blooded Romeo

"Another brilliant, fun read from Jenny Gardiner. The book is fun to read and I thoroughly enjoyed every word. Jenny Gardiner has put the fun back into romance books and I look forward to each book in this delightful series."
-- Anne Blyth

"I had planned on only reading a few chapters at first but couldn't put it down. A terrific storyline, well-developed and extremely relatable characters, what's not to love?? Great read!"
-- Samantha Reeves

Big O Romeo

"I could not put this book down. Warning don't start this book late at night as you will not want to stop reading.
-- Di

Sleeping with Ward Cleaver

"A fun, sassy read! A cross between Erma Bombeck and Candace Bushnell, reading Jenny Gardiner is like sinking your teeth into a chocolate cupcake...you just want more."
--Meg Cabot, NY Times bestselling author of Princess Diaries, Queen of Babble and more

Slim to None

"Jenny Gardiner has done it again--this fun, fast-paced book is a great summer read."
--Sarah Pekkanen, NY Times bestselling author of *The Opposite of Me*

Falling

for

Mr. No Way in Hell

(book three of the Falling for Mr. Wrong series)

by Jenny Gardiner

Chapter One

LACY Caldwell secured her long, tawny hair into a loose side braid, pulled her goggles over her bright green eyes, and tugged on the iridescent teal mermaid tail that had, like it or not, become an appendage she'd become oddly attached to over the past year. Since last January, Lacy had supplemented her income to pay for grad school by working as a mermaid at a cheesy roadside tiki bar in the small town of Verity Beach in North Carolina's Outer Banks.

At first, she simply took the job because it was a job to be had. She'd never aspired to be a freak attraction for tourists looking for a good laugh while getting drunk on too many beers. But then she surprised herself by finding out she kinda loved both the job and the quirky group of people she worked alongside at the Mermaid's Purse, too.

This included eighty-seven-year-old Edna Dingleheimer, who'd been pounding out customers' favorite tunes on the electric keyboard four nights a week since the year John Kennedy was assassinated. Despite her one-of-a-kind appearance (bleached-blond beehive hairdo, Coke-bottle-thick eyeglasses, knuckles knobbed with arthritis, and dressed in a grass skirt over a pair of blue jeans), Edna's presence always took second fiddle to the main attraction: two mermaids who dallied each night in a swimming pool on the other side of a large picture window that overlooked the dark, dank interior of the Mermaid's Purse Tiki Bar and Lounge.

Lacy could relate to how a stripper must feel. Whenever she worked, the many sets of leering eyes were laser focused on her, sometimes for hours at a time, though she was far more modestly garbed than a stripper. That said, the clamshell bra wasn't exactly a turtleneck, and she had large enough breasts that they couldn't help but spill out a little bit from the tiny confines of those hard cups.

Initially she'd felt self-conscious in her low-cut tail and that clamshell bikini top, but soon she realized it was fun getting paid (and earning some pretty generous tips) to flipper around a swimming pool for several hours a night. The exercise was an added bonus, and she had the quarter-bouncing abs to prove it. And since the pool was indoors, they weren't exposed to the elements, which was a huge plus.

The biggest downside was sheer boredom. You could only do so much in a mermaid tail—a few underwater flips here, a handful of turns there, a couple of tail slaps with whatever other mermaid was on duty that night, and maybe send some seductive bubble kisses to the people at the bar, and then you had to get creative. Thank goodness, she had to surface for air every twenty seconds or so—at least that provided a change of scenery.

Often Lacy stuck around after work for a late snack and to chat with her coworkers. She adored the owner,

Vera Cosmopolous, a seventy-something Greek American woman who it seemed had made it her life's goal to fatten Lacy up, even though Lacy felt plenty fattened enough already, thanks.

"Here," Vera said, sliding a plate with grilled pita and baba ghanoush, an eggplant and tahini dip, toward Lacy, who had to admit she was starved after four hours of swimming. "This will be good for you and will help you get over that stupid man."

The stupid man she was referring to was her now ex-boyfriend, Billy Crapple. Yes, that was his name, deservedly so. Although Billy "What a Complete Pile of" Crapple was what she preferred to call him nowadays. Lacy had devoted the past two years of her life to building a relationship with him, only to find out he'd been seeing not one, not two, but three different women at the same time. Three-timing Lacy. When she found that out—based on a phone call from one of the suspicious three-fers, accusing *her* of being the other woman—she kicked him to the curb, vowing to steer clear of men for the foreseeable future. From here on out, she was devoting herself to finishing up her degree and stockpiling money as a mermaid.

It was a good life. Or good enough, albeit a teensy bit lonely. Currently the biggest stressor in her world was the looming engagement party of her friend Carly, whose fiancé Jimmy was good friends with Billy. The last thing Lacy wanted to do was show up dateless with him in attendance.

"I tell you what you need, honey," Vera said as she helped herself to the pita bread she'd proffered to Lacy. Her electric green nail polish practically glowed in the

3

dim light of the bar as she pointed at her mermaid employee who'd become like a daughter to her. "You need to bring a man with you and show that crappy Billy Crapple you never looked back once he was in your rearview mirror."

Lacy sighed. "Yeah sure. Great idea. But who might you suggest?" She looked around the empty bar. "I mean I could bring Stan with me"—she nodded toward a regular leaning over the bar who was twice her age with a bushy walrus mustache, a bad toupee, and a wife at home—"but that wouldn't work on many levels."

They both laughed at the idea. Stan scowled at them.

"Can't you think of any man who might go, even as a pity date?"

Lacy rolled her eyes. Exactly what she wanted to be: a pity date. Even though that's precisely what she needed to find.

"I dunno," she said. "I mean there's this guy I keep noticing everywhere at the gym with these piercing blue eyes. He was next to me in yoga last week, and I've seen him at the other end of the room in boxing class now and then."

Vera shook her head. "As long as you didn't see him in ballet class, I say go for it."

"Like go for it as in, approach the guy whose name I don't even know, and say, 'Uh, hey. I'm sort of a loser and can't find a date and I need one badly to taunt my cheater ex-boyfriend and, well, we *did* do yoga together, so it's almost as if we know each other, so what say you be my platonic date?'"

Vera waved her hand, dismissing the cynical suggestion. "It's as good an approach as any. Unless you want to put an ad in the paper."

"No one puts ads in the paper anymore."

Vera shrugged. "Oh, excuse me. Then you can put a notice in Craigslist, and I'll hope and pray you aren't murdered in your sleep." She clasped the cross dangling from her neck.

"Fine, I get your drift. I should lose the shame and ask this guy. Even though I'm likely to see him every damned day at the gym, which will be perpetually humiliating if and when he turns me down."

Vera frowned. "Humiliating is when you're left at the altar with a bouquet of white tea roses and no fiancé. I speak from experience."

It always saddened Lacy that Vera never did marry after that episode. Instead she made the bar her life and family, and now here she should be retired and enjoying life, but with no one to share it with, she kept on working.

"You do know that guilt trip isn't going to work on me, lady." Lacy planted a fat kiss on Vera's cheek.

Only it *did* work every damned time she used that ploy. Each time Lacy thought about being alone and in her seventies, it almost prompted her to start looking for someone before she became an old and lonely spinster. If spinsters even existed anymore. Couple that with the need to prove to Billy that she'd long since moved on meant that she was indeed going to muster up the courage to ask her yoga buddy to be her date. Even if it killed her.

Chapter Two

CAMERON Sanders ran his fingers through his thick, wavy, dark hair, then wiped the sweat from his brow with one of those lousy, rough gym towels that felt like sandpaper on your skin. He knew he'd been hanging at the gym too much when he started to give a damn about the texture of sweat towels. That's what happens when you're a down-on-your-luck artist who makes diddly-squat sketching caricatures of tourists wandering the boardwalk.

It wasn't as if he wanted to be a professional kitsch artist, but man, it was hard making a living selling his real paintings. Art could be such a mercurial business. And now that the gallery he'd been featured in had shut down, he was back to practically selling shit out of the trunk of his car, which was so not how Leonardo da Vinci did it. Granted, Leonardo didn't have a car. But still.

Not that he was Leonardo. Or Michelangelo, for that matter. Or even that person who made the famous painting of the dogs playing poker. Perhaps he should have been doing commercial work like that dude, and then he wouldn't have so much free time to work out at the gym for hours at a time.

"Hi," he heard a voice say. "You mind if I join you?"

He looked to his right and saw no one on the machine next to him so he turned to the left and spotted that pretty girl he kept seeing in yoga class—the same one he dared set his mat next to last time in the hopes she'd notice him. She didn't.

He nodded. "Go right ahead, be my guest." He extended an arm in welcome, as if he controlled who did and did not get to use the StairMaster next to his.

He didn't want to creep on her, but he'd noticed her several times over the past month or so, and it had occurred to him that if only he had a steady income and a career he could crow about, he'd love to ask her out on a date. But shy of an overnight miracle, nothing in his life was going to change in the next, oh, forever. Which meant he'd better tuck away those fantasies until he might someday be able to employ them.

He stuck his earbuds in and returned to watching last night's episode of *The Bachelor*, which he only watched because, well, who wouldn't want twenty gorgeous women fawning all over you while you drink to your heart's content and go on awesome vacations? This was the closest he was gonna get to the fantasy.

A few minutes later he felt a tap on his shoulder. He looked over to see the woman with the deep emerald-green eyes, so soothing and damp they reminded him of a cool pine forest in the summertime. Last time her hair was in a high ponytail, but this time it was braided down her back. Either way, it made him think how amazing it would be to have a firm grip on her hair as he watched her mouth wrapping slowly around his cock. Which was jumping the gun a bit, since he hadn't even mustered up the courage to introduce himself, let alone invite her on a date. Nor would he, not with his depleting bank account and failing artistic career.

He glanced over at the woman who was waving and using some sign language to communicate with him. He removed an earbud.

She smiled. "Oh God, I'm so sorry to bother you, but I noticed you were watching *The Bachelor* and I totally missed it last night and wanted to watch it now but I forgot my earbuds and is there any chance you'd share one of yours with me? Working out is so boring otherwise with nothing to watch."

He shrugged. Couldn't hurt to give her one—as long as she could keep pace with him on the machine. And she looked plenty fit enough to do that. In fact, with those arms, it looked like she could kick his ass if need be and right hook him into the next century. Plus, that ass of hers was so perfectly shaped, just right to cup his hands around. And those legs. Well, shit, it didn't say much about him that all he could do was look at the woman and think how many different ways he might like to fuck her. Although wasn't that how every guy was? Nothing wrong with dreaming.

He handed her his left earbud and they started climbing again, and for the next twenty minutes, they climbed their stairs to nowhere together while indulging in someone else's fantasy world without actually being in it or conversing with each other about it. It was all very meta.

Cameron was about ready to bail on the stair-climbing, but every once in a while, he caught a great sidelong glimpse of her ass and that motivated him to keep on keeping on, at least for a few more minutes. Eventually she tapped him on his shoulder and offered up the earbud. It made him a little sad that their shared moment was drawing to a close.

"Hey," she said as her fingers pressed the earbud into the palm of his hand. "Thanks so much for sharing. I appreciate it."

He slowed down his machine till it came to a halt, then wiped his face again. "Sure thing," he said, taking a swig of water. "I was honored to share them with you."

She grinned. "Honored? Sheesh. I never knew it could be such a good thing for me to mooch gym supplies from someone. I'll have to get into the habit of that more often." She bent over, her hands on her knees, while she panted a little. Which of course got his blood going even more, since he'd love to hear more of her panting while bent over, with less clothes on and maybe even more sweat.

They stood facing each other behind their machines, dabbing off perspiration and catching their breaths.

"That thing about kills me," she said, placing her hand on her hip as she pointed a thumb at the StairMaster.

"Right? I feel like everyone else in here on those wimpy treadmills and stuff isn't getting nearly the workout we are."

"I'll go with that." She nodded, then extended her hand. "Hi. I'm Lacy, by the way. Lacy Caldwell."

He slid his palm to hers. "Cameron Sanders. You can call me Cam."

"It's great to finally meet you," she said. "I know we've been in a few of the same classes together. I think you were next to me at Vinyasa yoga the other day, right? And maybe boxing too?"

He nodded. "And don't forget Body Pump."

They laughed.

"Clearly we have shared interests," she said, glancing at her watch.

"You in a hurry to leave?" He nodded at the timepiece on her wrist.

She shook her head. "No, not at all. I have a class in an hour and wanted to be sure I had time to shower."

Well, crap. Now he was going to be obsessed with thoughts of her in the shower for the rest of the day.

"What a shame," he said. "I was going to see if you'd like to go grab some coffee."

She arched her brow. "Huh. Yeah, sorry, I don't have time for that now." She pinched her lips with her fingers as an idea emerged. "Though please forgive me if you think this is an odd suggestion, but I have another idea that might be a fun alternative. Bear with me." She held up her finger. "So, I'm only suggesting this because we're practically family now that we've shared earbuds and all." She grinned.

He loved her smile, those white teeth all nice and straight and perfect.

"You've got my attention," Cam said, wrinkling his brow. "And I hope you aren't asking me to join you to, say, visit your husband in jail."

She shook her head and held up her hand with a barren ring finger. "Oh, trust me. No husband. No way, no how." She dusted off her hands to get rid of that thought.

"I have to admit that's a bit of a relief." More than a bit, now that he'd put himself out there by asking her out for coffee.

"In that case, I hope you don't think this is terribly weird of me." She scuffed the toe of her sneakers along the carpeted gym floor as she stared downward.

"The longer you wait, the bigger chance I'm going to conjure up some bizarre scenario in my head and then that will be weirder still."

She shook out her hands and flexed her fingers as if she was trying to wake up a sleeping limb or warming up for a race of some sort. "Okay, here goes." She sucked in a breath. "So, you see, I have to go to this party and this ex-boyfriend, who is a total jerk, is going to be there, and I need to take someone—anyone—as long as he's male and has a pulse, though it doesn't hurt if he's good-looking, so that I don't look like a dateless loser, and I was wondering if maybe you'd be that person perhaps?"

Cam lifted an eyebrow, amused by her half-cocked invitation. He shook his head as if clearing his brain.

"So, let me get this straight. You need a prop. To make your ex-boyfriend jealous. And I'm as good a one as any. It's unclear as to whether I fall into the good-looking prop category or if I'm simply the man with a pulse." He cocked a brow in question.

She squinted. "That didn't come out so well, did it?"

He laughed and waved his hand. "Not to worry. I've got a tough hide, so I didn't take it personally."

"I'm sorry. I didn't mean to be rude."

"It wasn't rude at all. Just funny. In a peculiar way."

"Peculiar as in you're going to humor me and be my

date to Carly and Jimmy's engagement party, so Billy Crapple can see that I've moved on?"

He turned his head toward her. "Have you moved on?"

She ski-sloped her brows. "From Billy Crapple? Hell yeah. Believe me, there was no love lost there. I was happy to be rid of him. But I don't want him to think I can't land a man and I need him back or something."

He took another swig from his water bottle. "Well, that's completely preposterous. Obviously"—his gaze slowly scanned her from head to toe—"you could land any man you set your sights on."

She pointed at her red, sweaty face, strands of hair clinging to her forehead. "Yeah, especially right about now, all smelly and sweaty."

"I can assure you no man would be turned off by a sweaty woman." He grinned. "Quite the contrary, in fact." He didn't want to scare her off by being too suggestive, so he steered the conversation elsewhere. "But in answer to your question, I'd love to be your pulse."

She jumped up and clapped her hands. "Oh, yay. Thank you! And honestly, you're way more than a pulse—you are one hundred percent good-looking prop material."

Cameron had never been more thrilled to be used by a woman in his life.

Chapter Three

OOOH, snap. That had to have been one of the ballsier moves Lacy had made in a while, somehow persuading the stranger with the piercing blue eyes to accompany her to the engagement party. She was pretty proud of herself for taking a chance. It was scary, putting yourself out there like that. But he seemed nice and understanding. Besides, he shared his earbud with her. That was surely the sign of a kind man.

What was his name again? Cameron Sanders. Kind of a cute name. And she did love those eyes of his. Not to mention he filled out his gym clothes quite nicely. She'd kept trying to sneak a look at him when they were climbing their respective StairMasters.

Of course now she was worried that maybe they needed a preliminary date before the real fake date, so they didn't seem like they were on their first date pretending to actually know each other. It would be super embarrassing if Billy thought she dragged some guy along merely to show him up. Even though that's precisely what she was doing. Not that she cared what Billy thought. But still. If she were Billy she'd find that lame.

She exited class and raced over to the Mermaid's Purse for the late shift. Vera was going to be so proud of her. When she arrived at the lounge, she quickly changed into her "uniform" so she wasn't late getting into the pool.

The place was packed, which surprised her since it was already well after the dinner rush on a weeknight. Every table was filled and the bar didn't have a free seat. Sometimes she wished she could be that person relaxing at the retro-yet-authentic red Naugahyde-trimmed bar, chitchatting with friends. But she had bills to pay and a real life to attend to, so instead of being a patron, she was their entertainment. She'd been saddled with debt since her mother had become ill years earlier. After her mom passed, Lacy was able to do something for herself and return to school. But with that came tuition and books, and she now had to pay rent; since her mother's place ended up in foreclosure, there was no freeloading at home. She had learned quickly that adulting could sure take a toll on a girl.

She was glad to learn Meghan Clancy, a petite blonde she'd become friends with since working at the Purse, was on duty with her tonight. Though the only problem with wanting to work a shift with a friend when you swam on display for a living was that you didn't end up getting to talk. Sure you spent hours together, but underwater, mostly. Sort of a weird dynamic of the business. But all good.

Lacy decided to let her hair flow freely, since the tip of tonight's costume, a hot pink mermaid tail, had flowing tendrils that drifted behind her as her long locks did when she swam, lending an ethereal look. She gave a quick wave to Meghan, who was already in the water, and dove in. For the next four hours, the two of them glided through the water, sometimes playfully splashing each other, other times curling around each other's tails as they swam. Lacy was good at getting customers interested in her, sometimes simply by crooking her finger at one who seemed to be intently watching her. She'd then point to the tip jar that was along the bar and the customer often got the hint.

After their shift ended, Lacy and Meghan decided to stick around for a drink and some catching up. Lacy pulled her wet hair up into a bun and whatever patrons remained were none the wiser that she had been on the other side of the glass as their entertainment only minutes earlier.

"Okay so that guy with the long ZZ Top beard," Meghan said as she dragged her hands down off her chin in imitation.

"The one with the tattoos on his neck?" Lacy said, shivering.

"Yeah, him. He gave me the willies." She winced. "He kept pointing at me and beckoning for me to come near him."

"Ew." Lacy swept her hand across the counter in refusal. "No way. The good news is we're protected from creepy men by that glass wall. Besides, if you have a bad feeling, you have to listen to your gut."

"My gut told me I don't think we're compatible." She laughed and high-fived her friend.

It was true, being on exhibit as they were could be an uncomfortable proposition. Most customers were fine; many hardly noticed them swimming around after about five minutes. But sometimes, ugh, there were a few who mistook their entertainment value as a come-on or something.

"Speaking of going out with complete strangers…" Lacy cleared her throat.

Meghan lifted her brow. "Surely you're you not referring to yourself, are you?"

Lacy shrugged. "Sorta. I mean I set up a date for myself, but it's not an actual date."

"You mean for the engagement party?"

She pursed her lips. "Yeah. That. I mean I couldn't show up alone. That would seem like letting Billy win." She wagged her finger. "Not that this is a win-lose thing. Not like he could ever win on anything anyhow. But I didn't want him thinking I couldn't do better than him."

"Of course you can do better than him."

She nodded. "Right? It's only that I haven't tried. I mean who's got time, anyhow? I'm perfectly fine with my life right now, and to be honest, it's much, much better without him in it. But still."

"So, who's the mystery date?" Meghan leaned in for the answer.

"Is it the guy from ballet class?" Vera slipped down on a barstool next to Meghan and leaned over to join the conversation.

Lacy waved her hand. "Oh, stop. You know I don't do ballet."

"I had a customer tonight who told me you were like a prima ballerina."

"More like a prima donna," Meghan said, elbowing her friend in the ribs.

"Takes one to know one." Lacy winked.

16

"So, did you ask the gym rat?"

"You make him sound so desirable, Vera." Lacy rolled her eyes. "But yes, I got up the nerve to ask him and he said yes."

"He did? You have a date? Oh, honey, I'm so proud of you. This calls for a toast." She motioned for the bartender, a woman named Juno who was well into her sixties with tat-sleeved arms and the strong, set jaw of a boxer. "A round of ouzo for the ladies."

"Ouzo?" Lacy shook her head. "Vera—you know I can't drink that stuff. Don't you use it to clean your carburetor?" They all laughed as Vera handed out shot glasses to them.

"Enough of that nonsense." She clinked glasses with the others. "*Ya mas*. To your health."

"To your health, Vera," Lacy said. "And I mean that. I already lost one mother. I can't afford to lose my replacement mom."

Vera smiled. "Oh, doll. Don't you worry. I'm not going anywhere. Not for a good, long while."

"Promise?" Lacy said.

"Cross my heart and hope to die, honey."

They clinked their glasses against one another to seal the deal.

Chapter Four

LACY wanted to have control over this faux date, so she insisted on driving. It wasn't like she was an alpha dog or something. Rather she wanted to be able to call all the shots for the duration of the evening.

After returning from a daytime shift at the bar, she quickly dried her hair, securing it into a French braid, then slithered into an emerald-green slip dress she was pretty sure she'd never worn when she and Billy were an item. She put the finishing touches on her makeup and applied her favorite bright fuchsia lipstick, pressing her lips together to spread it evenly. With a quick nod of approval in the mirror, she grabbed her keys and purse, and got into the car.

She was perfectly willing to pick Cameron up at his place, but he insisted they meet at a coffee shop a few blocks from the gym, so she pulled up at 6:30 on the nose and found him looking remarkably handsome in a charcoal-gray suit and light blue shirt. She didn't even have time to get out of the car to greet him before he opened the passenger side door and got in.

"Oh! Hey!" she said, feeling a bit awkward to have this weird pickup locale for her non-date. It seemed unnatural to do things this way but being that it was already going to be an unorthodox type of night, oh well.

To make matters worse—how was she supposed to greet him? A quick wave from the driver's seat? No. That would be weird. And a hug was too awkward, what with having to bend over the center console and reach over the dashboard all gangly. Too much room for poking an eye or an inadvertent boob grab on his part. While she mentally ticked off her diminishing options, he answered the dilemma for her and leaned over and gave her a quick peck on the cheek.

"You look beautiful!" He smiled broadly as his eyes gave her a slow once-over.

Well, hmmm. This wasn't a real date. At least she didn't think it was. But it sure felt like it as his gaze settled on her breasts for a half beat longer than expected. She wished she could return the ogle because, well, judging from what she'd seen when he was standing in the doorway of Cuppa Joe, he sure cleaned up real nice himself. But that would be totally uncool. No gawking at the hired help. Not that he was hired, per se. But he was here to do a job, not as her newfound boy toy. Though if she were to have a newfound boy toy, he'd sure be a prime candidate. She always had a thing for a pair of mesmerizing deep, iris-blue eyes.

"You want to give me the lowdown on this thing we're going to, so I know what I've gotten myself into?" He grinned as he pointed a finger gun to his temple.

Lacy waved a hand. "Oh, no worries. It shouldn't be that bad. I mean it's an engagement party, and you won't know a soul there, so, yeah, on second thought, it might sort of suck for you."

"I'll know you though." He lifted his brows.

She looked at him and thrust out her lower lip. "Well, sorta, I guess." She shrugged. "I mean, after all, we do have a longtime relationship that involves strength, determination, and resolve." She was making this up as she went along. But technically that's how they met, working toward a common goal of fitness.

"Is that how we're going to play this one to everyone? Like we toughed it out climbing Mount Everest or something?" He gave her a wink.

"No!" She playfully slapped his hand. "I was kidding. But seriously, I guess we need to figure some of this out. We're supposed to be dating, right? So where did we meet?"

He glanced at her. "The more truth we stick with, the better," he said. "It's easier to remember that way. So, we met at the gym. I eyed you one day in those short shorts of yours—"

She rolled her eyes. "Let's be real here."

"I am being real. I did eye you in those short shorts. And I liked what I saw."

"I don't have any short shorts!"

He tipped his head down as if he didn't buy it. "The dark blue ones? Trimmed in pink?"

Lacy squinted her eyes. Crap. Those were the ones she only wore when all her laundry was dirty. "Okay, so fine. I do have that one pair. But I don't wear them very often."

"I think you should wear them every day."

"But they creep up my butt cheek—"

He nodded. "Now you're getting the idea."

Oh God. She wore too-small shorts and strangers

even noticed it. Worse still she was pretty sure she wore them in yoga, with all that bending and stuff. "I'm sorry. I'm so embarrassed about that." She shook her head to try to erase the memory.

He knit his brows. "Are you nuts? That is not something you should apologize for. I can assure you that I—and no doubt the entire male population of the gym—am particularly grateful for those shorts."

Lacy could feel her face go red and made a mental note to wear sweatpants to the gym next time. "Okay, then, enough about my ill-fitting gym wear. What else about how we met?"

"I invited you to grab coffee and you instead asked me to pretend to be your date at an engagement party."

She threw him a look. "Very funny. Let's go with this: we met in yoga over Sun Salutations. I complimented you on yours, and you, in turn, gave me pointers on improving my Tree Pose. The next thing we knew—"

"We were happily downward dogging together." He grinned. He had a beautiful smile. Even if his comment was awfully suggestive, considering they hardly knew each other.

"While I might on some level relish telling Billy that you and I have been locked in our very own little lovey-dovey Down Dog, I say let's not go there. Yet. I'm content for him to see that I've gotten over him and his untrustworthy ways and found a far better man."

"Okay, so no down dogging. Got it. Instead we started going out, hit it off, and voila, here we are at whose engagement party?"

"Carly's. Carly D'Agostino and I were roommates a

couple of years ago before I mistakenly moved in with Billy, and the rest is history there. When I was first dating Billy, Carly met his friend Jimmy Weinkopf, who she's now marrying. Billy and Jimmy played in this lame-ass garage band together."

"Ahhh… a boy band?"

She laughed. "That would be awesome if you asked Billy about his boy band. He'd probably try to punch you, though, so don't do that."

"A little sensitive?"

"I think it's that he knows they're not very good, and to be honest I've heard better drummers in an elementary school marching band. He's thin-skinned about it because they suck." She laughed.

"He sounds like a real winner." Cameron cocked an eyebrow at her.

She frowned. "Yeah, he doesn't come across so great. I think he started out nice, and I was intrigued by his musical interests at first. Until I realized they were a bit lacking." She paused, lost in thought. "He was sweet and friendly, and I don't know… I hadn't dated a ton of guys and he paid attention to me, which sounds super lame now that I've uttered those words."

"If that's why you dated him for so long—because he paid attention to you—then I hate to break it to you but you are selling yourself short. You absolutely deserve way better than a guy who yanks you around and fools around with other women while he's living with you."

Lacy heaved a sigh. "Look, it's complicated. I'd recently lost my mom, and I was sharing an efficiency with Carly that was over the garage of some random person's house because the rent was super cheap and—"

She furled her brow. "Okay, I'll admit it. I was lonely. I needed someone to lean on. Sometimes when you're lonely, you don't even realize it, but you lower your standards. Which I freely admit I did with Billy."

Cameron held his hands up in surrender. "I'm sorry—I didn't mean to make you feel defensive. I guess I get a little too curious trying to figure out what motivates people. I mean here you are, you're a beautiful woman. You should be able to get any guy you choose."

"If it's any consolation, I did ultimately figure it out and grow a spine and ditch him." She clicked her turn signal as she steered onto a side street. They were heading to Carly's parents' house for this party, in a ritzy section of Verity Beach filled with oversized McMansions that Lacy could only dream of owning someday.

"I'm glad you realized you deserved better. And I'm sorry if I picked open a scab."

She let out a small laugh. "I think you should tell Billy that he's a scab, too. A scab with a boy band. It would do my heart wonders."

"Don't you worry your pretty little head about ole Billy-boy. I know exactly how to handle him. Leave all the talking to me."

On the one hand, that sounded like such a nice, easy solution. On the other hand, a sense of dread came over her at the thought. All the things that could possibly go wrong in that scenario raced through her head. As she glanced over at her "date," her gut told her this night might well spin out of her control no matter how much control she thought she wielded over it.

Chapter Five

BILLY Crapple is a douchebag. That was the thought that kept running through Cam's head as he reached for Lacy's hand and they approached the large yellow contemporary house that occupied a hell of a lot of real estate on this stretch of Verity Beach. He couldn't see the point of two people taking up six thousand square feet of space in a house and the commensurate land surrounding it. But whatever. The upside is folks who could afford a huge house on the ocean would no doubt be serving top-shelf liquor at this party, and a fat finger of Knob Creek bourbon would not be a bad idea to help break the ice. Because he wanted to put on a good show for his audience and help Lacy redeem herself with that prick of an ex-boyfriend of hers, a little social lubricant was definitely called for.

As they got to the door and Lacy reached to ring the bell, he turned toward her and clasped her hand with both of his, pulling her toward him.

"I promise I will be the best fake date you've ever had, Lacy, uh, what did you say your last name was again?"

She grinned. "Caldwell. You'd better at least

remember that much."

"If we're sleeping together, I need to know your last name."

"I don't think we need to get so granular with information tonight. Let's stick with the 'we're dating' bit and leave the rest to their imaginations."

"Your wish is my command, milady." He took a bow and stepped back as the door opened and Carly's mother greeted the two.

"Lacy!" She reached out and enveloped her in a bear hug. "It's been ages! So glad you could make it." She paused and turned to Cam, nodding her head. "And this is your mystery man who Carly was telling me about?"

"Yes, this is Cameron. Thanks for letting me bring him along tonight. He was so excited to meet Carly and Jimmy."

"And I know Carly's excited to meet your new fellow. Come along. Let's get you two some drinks, and you can mingle and find the lovebirds."

"And here I thought you were referring to Lacy and me when you said lovebirds," Cameron said, pulling Lacy in for a hard squeeze. He was going to lay it on thick, starting with the mom and working his way down the line. He knew from personal experience that moms had the biggest bullshit detectors going, so if she believed him, everyone would.

Cameron handed Lacy a glass of white wine and they clinked glasses.

"Here's to new lovers," he said, winking. Lacy choked on her wine.

"You don't have to fake it with me, you know." She wiped her dribble of wine from her mouth with a cocktail napkin. "Save it for everyone else."

"I wanted to get some practice in."

Lacy's eyes opened wide. "Oh my God. I forgot to ask you anything about you. What am I supposed to say if someone asks me about you?"

"Easy enough. Steer the conversation back to you. Or to them."

"But I don't even know what you do for a living. Do you have a job?"

He grimaced. "That's complicated."

"Complicated? Either you have one, or you don't."

"Well there's the job that I'm doing and the job I was doing and the job I want to be doing."

"What's behind door number three?"

"What I want to be doing?" He laughed.

"Any information you can share would be helpful."

"Fine, but you might want to pull up a seat. This might take awhile."

"We've got all night."

"Okay, so I'm an artist." He shrugged. "Sometimes I feel the need to apologize for that, as if it's a dirty thing, even though I know it's not. My preferred medium is watercolors. I paint landscapes, often beach scenes but not always."

"That's cool. I've always admired someone who can see something and translate it to canvas with their hands

26

and a brush. What an amazing skill."

"Well, it might be cooler if I could make a living that way. I was finally on the cusp of breaking through. A local gallery had showcased my work and several of my larger drawings even sold, which was pretty sweet. But then they went out of business." He frowned.

Lacy knit her brow. "Oh, that sucks."

"It super sucks."

"So, what'd you do?"

"First I got good and drunk and lamented that I didn't get an MBA like my brother Peter. He's joined the robber baron class on Wall Street and makes millions a year for doing nothing but gambling on the stock market."

Lacy reached out and flicked a piece of fuzz from his lapel. "Yeah, but people like that, they're nothing like artists, who have amazing talent and a way to see the world that is so much more intense, and honestly, so much more valuable."

He shook his head. "Unfortunately, vision doesn't pay the rent." If only she knew the hovel he was living in to save money, she'd turn and run the other way, screaming. Beautiful women like Lacy didn't settle for men who chose capricious career paths.

She laughed. "Don't I know it!"

"Which reminds me—I have no idea what you do either."

"I'm probably not far above you in the pay scale department. I've been working to finish up my graduate degree."

"Oh, really? What are you studying?"

"Urban planning. I'm a bit of a community geek. I

love the idea of preserving and restoring areas in a way that maintains the culture and integrity of the community."

"Huh. I guess I've never given that any thought."

"For instance—did you know when the interstate highways were created in this country, they were often deliberately built in poor neighborhoods, destroying long-held communities in the process? That alone has helped perpetuate and reinforce the cycle of poverty in many poor, black, and blue-collar communities throughout this country." When she started talking about issues like this her hands became animated, flitting rapidly through the air, emphasizing her points. "And you can understand why, all of a sudden, your neighbors are separated, their houses taken by the government so that highways could be constructed smack-dab in the middle of your neighborhood. Friends and family got split up, and the lives they knew were undone." She shook her head. "To me this is what we need to fix when possible and avoid at all costs. No one should have to go through what happened back then."

"I had no idea those things occurred. That's horrible."

She nodded. "It *is* horrible. Worse still that it was a deliberate policy of the government. And it happened in every major city in this country: New York, Miami, Los Angeles, Seattle, Baltimore. The list goes on. I think it's important to maintain the cultural integrity of a community and it's what I hope to do eventually. If and when I finish school."

"Not if, but when," he said, holding his finger up. "I can tell you've got the determination to get there and I'm rooting for you."

Leaning over, he kissed her on the cheek and she blushed. "What was that for?"

He pressed his mouth to her ear. "Don't look now but there's a troglodyte of a man nearby who seems to be staring at you as if you're a saber-toothed tiger steak he wants to dig into."

She laughed. "Is that what troglodytes ate?"

He shrugged. "I haven't a clue, but it sounded good." He reached out and grabbed her hand in his, lacing their fingers together as he placed a soft kiss on her knuckles. "He keeps staring at you, so I feel it's safe to assume that's the asshole you mistakenly gave your heart to?"

Her back was to the man, so Cam gave her a color commentary.

"So, he looks like he just hopped out of a WWE ring after a steroid bender. He's wearing a pair of tight-fitting hipster pants that make him look like an idiot." He leaned in. "Everyone knows hipster pants are only for slender men, not studio wrestlers. Also he's wearing flip-flops, another faux pas, particularly considering the event, not to mention the lack of style. And a too-tight black tee."

Lacy rolled her eyes. "Ugh. I'm sure it's Billy. What do I do?"

Cameron set his drink down on a nearby windowsill and leaned forward, his hand gently cupping Lacy's chin.

"What else can we do but this?" he said, as he lowered his mouth and settled his lips on hers.

Chapter Six

OMIGOD omigod omigod. Lacy couldn't believe she was standing in Carly D'Agostino's parents' sunroom while the cute guy with the gorgeous eyes and nice butt from the gym was suddenly tracing his lips and tongue along her lips as if they belonged there. For that matter, she couldn't believe they *felt* like they belonged there, like no kiss she'd ever experienced before. But what the hell was she doing, going all-out PDA like this—at Carly's engagement party, no less? She wasn't even sure if it actually was Billy Crapple leering at her, yet here she was sucking face with her fake date in case it was. But if it was Crappie Crapple, oh Lord, what a wonderful way to announce to him that she had found far bigger fish to fry. Or kiss.

Although she was decidedly not kissing a fish. No, indeedy. She was kissing, make that being kissed by, a gorgeous man whose lips were soft and gentle against hers, whose tongue had somehow persuaded her—when, she couldn't quite say—to open her mouth and let him in to play a little with her own evidently needy tongue, based on how enthusiastically it received its unexpected caller.

Sheesh. It had been so long since she'd kissed a man, she'd have bet money she'd forgotten how to do it. But it was like riding a bike. A tall, dark, handsome bike—not some measly set of training wheels in hipster pants.

She needed to yield to the moment and not think about anything more than the feel of his tongue as it traced a path through her mouth, across the edge of her teeth, and along her own tongue, allowing her the decidedly erotic pleasure of tasting his mouth, a pleasant combination of bourbon and cinnamon and hints of things to come. She moaned.

She wasn't sure how loud it was and hoped to God that Carly's grandma—who she'd last noticed was about ten feet away from her, her hands resting on her walker, talking to the minister from her church—didn't pick up on what Lacy was in the midst of. Ack! If her grandma saw her going at it like a dog in heat with Cameron, Lacy would about die. Except who could think about dying of embarrassment when she was more likely to die of horniness because damn, this guy's kiss was stirring up some nascent sensations deep in her pelvis. Right now, she wanted nothing more than to squirm and press her body up against him like a lint brush to a pair of velvet pants covered in cat fur.

She closed her eyes and, in her unseeing state, fumbled to set down her wineglass, finding some nearby surface, thank God, as that freed up her hands to join in the fun. Hmmm… would it be deeply inappropriate if she hooked one leg around his waist so she could coax that body of his a little closer and line up her Slot A so he could simulate inserting his Tab B right *there*? Oh, crap, that would be such a bad idea. How could she even entertain such a thought? She settled for the safer alternative, which was to weave her fingers through his wavy dark hair as she angled her mouth more conveniently to absorb his kiss just so.

Damn, that man could kiss. Lacy wondered if there was an empty room in this house where they could maybe slip away to satisfy her embarrassingly carnal urges, but then she realized she didn't even know the guy she was kissing, so of course she wasn't going to sneak away for a quickie with him. At her friend's parents' house, no less. At said friend's engagement party. She needed to get a grip and fast because she was losing control quicker than a mom overseeing a slumber party full of tweens.

Think. Think think think think. Okay, so you're sucking face with Cameron. Your date. He's here to shove it in the face of Billy. Well, also to keep you from showing up alone. So, what's the best way to do that, other than grinding on him like it's the last dance at the prom and the lights will go on any minute?

Against her better judgment—make that her deeper desires—Lacy pressed her hands to Cameron's chest. And not to feel the contours of his solid pectoral muscles. They felt pretty damned perfect, and only made her wonder how it would feel to graze her fingers along his biceps, slipping them under his arms and stroking the hair beneath his underarms—for some reason she suddenly had the overwhelming need to do that.

Focus, Lacy.

With the most unnatural and cursed willpower, she broke the kiss at last, her heart beating double time in her chest as her eyes fluttered open to find his piercing blue ones locked on hers. For a moment, she thought she might actually faint from the intensity of it all.

Cameron leaned in and whispered into her ear, "How'd I do?"

Lacy blanched.

How'd I do? *How'd I do?* Ugh, talk about dumping a bucket of ice water over her head. Although maybe that was for the better: she needed this reminder that this was, indeed, merely a performance. Part of his job as her faux date tonight. Nothing more. Nothing less.

She dragged the back of her hand across her lips, wiping away any telltale moisture from what she mistakenly took for a heated kiss, then tugged her dress down with both hands as she collected herself and pasted a huge smile—the kind that hurts—across her face.

"Great!" she said, shaking her head for emphasis like a dopey cheerleader rooting for the quarterback to score the winning touchdown, even after he'd told her she was a fat pig. She reached for her wineglass and pulled it quickly to her lips and took a fat gulp, so big it was painful going down her throat. "Your performance was absolutely great."

Chapter Seven

PERFORMANCE? She thought his kiss was an act? Was she crazy? Although damn, what exactly was going on with him? Sure, he was interested in Lacy—after all, she was beautiful, had a great body, not to mention amazing tits (which he regretted not being able to palm during that little, um, performance).

And she seemed sweet enough. Plus he felt bad that this dickhead had dissed her so famously. But it's not like Cam was looking for anything with anyone right now. He could barely deal with his own issues these days, what with his crap job and crappier apartment—if you could call it that, considering it was a room in someone's guest cottage—and of course his crap state of mind in general. To be honest, he needed to focus on how to afford his gym membership next month, not to mention how to earn a living once high season ended and there weren't tourists here to have their silly pictures drawn as souvenirs. Maybe he'd have to find a job illiustrating crime scene sketches. Surely that business must always be bustling. Regardless, he didn't have time to court the likes of Lacy—what was her last name? Caldwell?—who honestly deserved someone better than him.

Cameron had a hard time drawing his gaze away from Lacy's sparkling green eyes—they were the eyes you'd see on a mermaid, he was certain of that. But when he did pull away he couldn't help but glance down at those amazing tits, and it was impossible not to notice her erect nipples standing at proud attention. No doubt waiting for his mouth to finish the empty promises he'd made only minutes earlier—to plant soft kisses along her jawline and lick his way down the column of her throat, his tongue drawing the fastest line to her breasts. He would first nip at those hard pebbles through her silky dress with gentle teeth, then slip the spaghetti straps down so his lips could fasten around her dusky areola and distended nipple, and he could suck and lick till she moaned with pleasure.

Pleasure. Fuck. He was a random guest at someone's engagement party and had spent the past however many minutes diddling his date. And now, it was abundantly clear to not only him but to that minister with the white collar standing close by that he was sporting a raging hard-on with absolutely zero chance of being relieved of it in the next four hours—or four weeks for that matter. Because it's not like Lacy was going to run out of here with him and find a cozy spot on his pull-out sofa. No chance she would suddenly decide that even if she didn't know him, she was going to sit on his cock and grind onto him until they exploded in a shared orgasm that would have him seeing stars.

He took a deep, cleansing breath, the way they instruct you to do in yoga, and thought of the most unpleasant thing he could imagine to try to tamp down the erection that was straining against his suit pants. His suit pants: the perfect launching point to bring him down. Because they made him think of his father, a retired naval captain, who bought him the suit in the hopes it would encourage him to interview for what he called "real" jobs. And when Cam told him that his real job involved making art, his father told him that was it, don't come looking to him for help or a place to stay or anything. If he was going to "chase foolish pursuits," well, then, he was on his own. Annnddd that thought masterfully killed the earlier joy in his cock, hopefully before the whole cocktail party started pointing at him and laughing.

"Well if it isn't Lacy Caldwell," he heard someone say as he fumbled for the tumbler of bourbon he desperately needed to swill from.

He heard Lacy clear her throat. "Uh, Billy?"

"You say that like you don't remember me," he said with a laugh. "We did live together, so I'd like to think you still recall some of the good times we had."

Lacy tugged on Cameron's arm and he turned in her direction. "Cameron, this is someone I went out with for a short while. Billy Crapple. Billy, this is my boyfriend, Cameron."

Billy Crapple sized Cameron up then turned to Lacy. "I always warned you that you couldn't get any better than me."

Cameron spat his drink into his glass. What a piece of shit. On so many levels.

"Oh, babe," Cam said, folding his hand into Lacy's. "Is this the guy you mentioned who had that really tiny dick, so small you couldn't even feel it inside of you?"

It was Lacy's turn to spit-take, and hers wasn't quite so graceful, splattering wine on Billy's black tee. Shame it wouldn't stain it.

She looked up at Cam through her lashes and smiled. "Huh. I wasn't even sure if I ever mentioned him to you, but I guess I did."

"Dude," Cameron said, extending his hand to Billy. "Great to meet you. And, well, hey, sorry." He looked down toward Billy's crotch. "Nothing you can do about that."

Billy glared at the two of them. "Fuck you, asshole," he said to Cameron, who tugged Lacy a little closer to keep her safe in case the idiot lost his temper. He struck Cam as the type of guy who would throw a drink in a woman's face with no compunction.

"Thanks for the offer, but I'd rather make love with my girlfriend here if it's all the same to you. She loves my huge cock." He put his arm around Lacy and led her out the nearby sliding glass door and away from the prying eyes of Billy Crapple.

Chapter Eight

"WELL," Lacy said as she drove away from the D'Agostinos' house. "I'd say mission accomplished back there."

She high-fived Cameron then flicked on her turn signal to leave the gated development and get out onto the main beach road. She was still marveling at how quick on his feet Cameron was with Billy, who was your average lunkheaded mouth breather, for the most part. He couldn't come up with a sudden putdown if it plunked itself on his lap and played with his little dick.

"We did a great job, didn't we?"

"I can't thank you enough for that." She grinned.

"Oh, you deserve kudos yourself," he said. "That near grope-and-grab session we had in front of him deserved an award."

"Best actor in a dramatic role?" She lifted a brow and hoped he would deny that acting had anything to do with it.

"Best leading lady, without a doubt." He winked at her. Crap. It was only an act, darn it.

Lacy was a little worried that Cam had laid it on too thick—that whole conversation about the size of their respective Johnsons... Oy. That wasn't usually conversation she would offer up. But, since he did it, it was sort of a beautiful thing. Got the point across and humiliated that louse of an ex of hers. Done and done.

"I'd say let's go get a drink but we already did that," Lacy said, wishing she could figure out a way they could resume where they left off when they were so rudely interrupted by reality.

Cameron yawned. "Thanks, but I probably need to call it a night."

Disappointment seeped through her. It was so weird—he seemed as into that kiss as she had been. But clearly he wasn't, so she needed to accept it and move on. "Sure. Can I drop you at home at least?"

He shook his head. "Right where you picked me up is fine."

Okay then... To avoid the awkward silence for the rest of the drive, Lacy cranked up the radio. She hated weird moments like this, not knowing what to say. Well, wanting to say something that would be potentially misinterpreted. So instead she said nothing. She pulled up to Cuppa Joe and put the car in park.

"You sure you don't need a ride?"

Cameron shook his head. "I'm good, thanks."

"Great. Uh, well, thanks so much for your help tonight. You were really amazing. I mean it was really amazing." Lacy blushed. "I mean what you did was amazing."

Oh God, did he think she meant the kiss? Not the comments? Should she clarify? Or would that make it worse?

He cocked his head and smiled. "Right back atcha.

You were pretty darned incredible yourself. I hope I gave you what you needed."

Well, er, um, not exactly, she wanted to say. *Because what I need is a Big O, which I haven't had, courtesy of a man, in, like six thousand years.* The sad reality was that Billy Crapple wasn't so good at servicing anyone but himself. All roads led to Billy when it came to sex. Lacy had been in so few relationships, she hadn't appreciated how very one-sided things were with him. But once she was done with him, she realized that she was perfectly fine with her little toy chest to help do the trick when the need came knocking. She hardly missed sex with *that* man, but she did indeed miss having sex with *a* man. Not that she was about to have sex with this man. After all, as she'd reminded herself several times already this evening, she didn't even know him. Shame, that.

"So, uh, maybe we can get together sometime soon?" Wait. Did she ask him out on another date? Had she truly ushered her pride out the back door once again? "I mean, I know we'll probably see each other at the gym, so it's not like—"

Cameron reached across the console and pulled her head closer to his, once again settling his lips on hers. This time it took no persuasion for her to open her mouth to him as she angled her head for better access and her tongue stroked his and their teeth clashed in the momentary haze of passion. Lacy could barely catch her breath, her heart was beating so hard in her chest. She wished she had it in her to be the aggressor, to move her hands from his hair, where she naturally slid her fingers, to his shoulders, his arms, even lower. Cameron seemed to be in Boy Scout mode, not daring to move anywhere below her neck. Where was her audacity when she needed it, darn it?

As quickly as he started the kiss, he ended it, pressing his forehead to hers as they both caught their breaths, then reaching for the handle of the car door.

"I'd like that very much, Lacy Caldwell," he said as he opened the door and slipped out into the warm night breeze.

Chapter Nine

I'D like that very much. I'd like that very much. I'd fucking like that very fucking much, you dumb piece of shit.

Cameron stood in front of the mirror making faces at himself as he mocked his complete cowardice when he had an obvious entrée to going further with Lacy than that wimpy kiss. But instead, he politely acknowledged that he'd like "something," not even specifying what that something was. He'd like another date? He'd like a cup of tea? He'd like to see her at the gym? He'd like to have buried three fingers inside her warm, wet center because he knew she was as hot for him as he was for her—he could tell by the kiss, by the way her breath came in short bursts. By the way her cheeks were flushed and the exposed skin on her chest even more so.

And yet he chickened out. *What happened to your mojo, man?* For Cam, it used to be as easy as breathing, making the moves on a woman. But now he was plunged headlong into some weird crisis of confidence that seemed to render him incapable of running the ball into the end zone. Instead he insisted on fumbling it so badly that now he didn't even know if he was going to go out with Lacy again or wave to her at the gym next time they ran into each other.

He knew one thing for certain: next time they did a yoga class together, he was, without a doubt, spreading his mat out behind her. When she went into Downward Dog, he could steal a peek or two at what he was missing out on, due to his own pathetic chickenshitism. And he was going to have to wear loose sweatpants to hide his rock-hard erection, natch. Fuck.

After Lacy dropped him at the coffee shop, he waited till she pulled back onto the main road, then walked to the far side of the parking lot and got into his car. From there, he drove the quarter mile or so to his lonely rental room, super bummed that he wasn't in a place in his life where he could have invited her back with him—even if it was only to talk, nothing else. He wouldn't invite a woman here to even ring the doorbell. Dammit, his luck needed to change, and fast.

"Oh shit, he seriously talked about him having a small penis?"

Lacy had finished working a lunch shift and was sitting at the bar with Vera and Meghan.

"Someone say something about a small penis?" The three of them looked over to see that Edna had just arrived.

"You always find the best time to join in the

conversation," Vera said as she went to the Bunn burner and poured a cup of coffee for her longtime keyboardist.

"Honey I've been around a long time and seen a lot of penises, so if you have any questions feel free to ask me." Edna reached for her coffee mug, her gnarled fingers wrapping around the container as she blew on it to cool it down a bit.

"Edna, I wouldn't have pegged you as a gal who got around a lot," Lacy said with a laugh.

Edna waved her hand. "Lordy, when you've lived as long as I have, you can't help but be exposed to more than your fair share of *that*."

Meghan's eyes grew wide. "Edna, hearing you say these things would be like my nanna talking to me about sex. I'm not sure that I can listen to this."

"I bet your nanna's even younger than me, so I could probably teach her a thing or two." Edna turned toward Lacy, who was nursing the beer Vera had poured for her. Lacy had schoolwork to do when she got home so was only having but a sip or two to be polite. Vera had brought her a plate of chicken souvlaki that tasted like she'd died and gone to Mykonos. She gladly inhaled that. What would she do without Vera taking care of her? She'd grown to love her as if she was her own mother over the past many months. Sometimes she felt guilty for not reciprocating her TLC more than she did. Though she did take Vera shopping and to the movies. They went out dancing for girls' night once a month with the other mermaids, and the two shared their favorite books on a regular basis.

Edna put her hand over Lacy's and continued her discussion. "So, what's this I hear about your man not being well-endowed?"

Lacy burst out laughing. "Oh, Edna, I don't even have a man! Which I guess means my man is not well-endowed in the least, being that he's nonexistent. Although my last man was, shall we say, relatively unimpressive."

Edna took a sip of her coffee, her thick eyeglass lenses steaming up as she drank. Her beehive seemed like it wanted to topple, like a Jenga tower with a dangling wooden block. "In that case, take my advice and hold out for a man who can please you down there." She pointed toward her crotch. "Because by God, you'll be stuck with him forever and if he's got one of those microscopic things you need a magnifying glass to find, well I can assure you you'll live to regret that."

Vera gave Lacy a side-glance and they all giggled.

"What happens if I fall for a guy only to learn too late that he's lacking *down there*?" Lacy said.

"That's why you need to sleep with him before you fall in love. That way, you know what you're buying into."

"Edna, that seems a little mercenary," Meghan said.

"Mercenary, schmercenary." She waved her hands again. "Would you buy a house without a home inspection?"

"No, but—"

"That's right. No buts. In this day and age, there is no reason to make a long-term investment without knowing what you're buying is all I'm saying. Look under the hood. Take a test-drive. At least take it around the block once or twice."

"As opposed to being the little old lady who ends up

only driving it to church on Sundays?" Vera said, poking Edna in the ribs.

"That's exactly what I'm saying. Why do you think she only took it out so rarely? The last thing you want is buyer's remorse when it comes to the man you're going to be having sex with for the next sixty years. Agreed, ladies?"

They all nodded at that. Sage advice from someone who'd been around the block a whole lot longer than the rest of them.

Which got Lacy thinking... If she even had another date with Cameron, should she throw caution to the wind and go for it? After all, it was awfully hard to go against advice from a wise elder.

Chapter Ten

YOGA class and two boxing classes came and went with no Lacy to be found. Cam tried to pretend he wasn't disappointed, but he'd be lying if he said he wasn't super bummed. He hadn't been able to get Lacy out of his mind for the past three days, and the commensurate blue balls that came with that mild obsession wasn't making things easier. The two-fingered tango was only a temporary remedy, it seemed. He'd flogged the dolphin the last thing before he went to bed and the first thing in the morning each day since they'd kissed. And each time he did so, he tormented himself thinking about what it would have been like to follow through on their empty wishes. What if he could have hastened her up to some bedroom on the second floor? He could have lifted that sexy-as-hell dress with those hardened nipples poking through, which left little to the imagination, and had his happy way with her.

It would have been a toss-up if he'd have started with those gorgeous breasts or instead slipped his fingers beneath the edge of her damp panties. He knew they'd be damp; she was feeling it as much as he was, of that he was sure. The thought that he might have slid his fingers through her slick juices and pressed them up into her center, bringing her to climax before she even knew what hit her about killed him with regret.

He was spending the afternoon working at a local arts collaborative, trying to find inspiration to paint something new, but it was so freaking hard to be creative when your mind went to one place and one place only. He gave half a mind to starting work on a series he'd call Snatch: watercolor paintings of vaginas, being that his brain seemed to have been freeze-framed on one woman's in particular, not that he'd had any contact with the damned thing. Maybe that's where the money would be for him, anyhow. Fine art erotica. Couldn't sell much worse than his landscapes at this point. The only problem would be tamping down a perpetual hard-on while trying to work on those paintings—it would be nigh impossible.

The door opened and he turned to see his artist friend Jamie Lundquist enter. He and Jamie had been friends in kindergarten, back when Cam originally lived in Verity Beach. Growing up as a navy brat, he didn't live in one place for too long. He'd lived there twice during his childhood—first when he was five and again when he was fifteen. His rootless existence didn't help establish many lifelong friends, so the fact that he and Jamie remained friends was important to him and was the reason he returned to Verity Beach during the summers while he was in college. It had been the only draw to return here—working at Jamie's mom's art gallery. Which was where he was able to place his own work at last. That is, until her parents split up and her mom had to sell the shop.

Jamie, with her sun-kissed blond hair and lean,

strong surfer-girl physique, had a California girl-next-door kind of face—warm brown eyes and a friendly smile. She had a cute diamond stud in her nose and almost always wore her hair in a messy bun or a ponytail since she spent so much time in the water.

Although they'd been great friends over the years, neither had any interest in the other beyond that. Jamie tended to go for the rowdy surfer type of guy, and Cam tended to be more understated, so he would never be her cup of tea. He was happy their friendship had survived so many years apart, made all the more wonderful in that she so appreciated his art and was making a living as a potter herself.

"What up, dude?" Jamie said, holding her hand up for a fist bump.

"Dudette, what's happening?"

Jamie leaned over his canvas, trying to see what he was working on.

"Probably more with me than you, judging by this piece of crap here." She poked him in the ribs. "Just giving you some shit."

He frowned. "Crap. I knew it wasn't my best work but didn't think it was that horrible."

"It's not horrible, but it's not, well, your best work."

She walked to the other side to try to get a different perspective, crossing her arms as she stared at it, frowning.

"The look on your face is telling me everything I need to know." He sighed and dropped his paintbrush. "I can't seem to muster up the creative juices to make anything that's more than adequate."

She put her hand to her chin. "Yeah, sorry, Cam. I'm

not feeling it with this piece. What's got you so blocked?"

He arched an eyebrow. "Life?"

She laughed. "Shit, tell me about it. My parents' divorce is about killing me. I am wondering if I can divorce the two of them and be done with their nonsense."

"That bad, huh?"

"Ugh." She rolled her eyes. "The last thing to sell is my folks' place, and they have a buyer. I've gotta be out of there in a couple of weeks. My childhood has to be packed up lock, stock, and barrel and I'm going to be homeless."

"You wanna be homeless together?"

"Where would we go?"

"Maybe set up a couple of refrigerator boxes underneath the boardwalk? We could camp out on the beach, build bonfires at night."

"Brilliant idea. Except there's a city ordinance against sleeping under the boardwalk." She thrust out her lower lip in a pout. "Probably to keep the likes of us from moving in permanently."

"That's about the best I can afford on my current pauper's wages. Guess I'll have to stay in the dreaded rental room for the rest of my life."

"Well, that doesn't make any sense. Why don't you move in with me?"

"You're moving out of your parents' place, remember?"

"Yeah, so when I said I was homeless, I meant I was without my family home. I'm not broke. It means I have to find a place to live. And my dad feels guilty, so he's buying me a little cottage. I've been looking at some houses over on Blue Heron Road—right across the street from the beach. I was going to have to start asking around for a roommate, but damn, I hadn't even thought of you."

"You're serious? I could move in with you?"

"As long as you agree to make some kick-ass paintings for the walls."

"I can't afford a lot of rent."

"Did you not hear the part about my father's buying me a cottage? I mean finding someone to pitch in for the rent is good and all, but I'm more concerned about having someone who's not a psycho as a roommate. Having you there would be perfect."

Cameron threw his shoulders back. A huge load had been lifted. "Wow, James. You seriously made my day. Now if only I could get my painting mojo back I'd be golden."

"Can't imagine what else would be holding you back. Unless maybe it was a girl." She pressed her finger into his chest for emphasis.

Cameron frowned.

"Oh, wow! I was kidding, but it is a girl, isn't it? Who is it? Tell me more. I need all the gory details."

Cameron sighed. "I wish there were gory details. It was all lead-up and no follow-through. Left me kicking myself for being such a coward."

"I didn't even know there was someone you were interested in. You need to spill."

"Okay, okay. Long story short: it's a girl at the gym. We've done classes together. She's cute and sweet. She needed a fake date for some event her slimy ex-boyfriend would be at. I was the fake date. To be convincing, I had to fake kiss her in front of the guy. Only it wasn't so fake once things got underway."

Jamie clapped her hands. "This is excellent. You have so needed to get laid for a long time. I mean, right?"

Cameron looked up from his attempts at painting to throw her a dirty look. "Honestly? Things are bad enough. Do we have to perform an autopsy on my sex life?"

"Only way to find the cause of death."

"I'd like to think it's more in a state of hibernation."

"All I know is when you aren't getting any, you get cranky, and boy have you been surly lately."

"And it looks as if I'm going to continue being surly because there is no chance of anything for the foreseeable future."

"Cloudy with a chance of blue balls?" She poked him in the ribs and started laughing.

"You don't know the half of it."

"So, where's this girl? Why don't you ask her out on a real date?"

"Because my life sucks and I live in a rental room owned by someone's grandma and I'm making shit for a living and the gallery that was exhibiting my paintings got sold in a divorce and—"

"Seriously I am going to yell at my mother about that again. That was so bogus of her to kneecap you like that."

"In her defense, I don't think my art career was on her mind at the time."

"No. But still." Jamie scratched her chin between her thumb and forefinger. "Where can we find this Cinderella of yours? You need to try for another chance with her. I mean you like her right?"

"Of course I do. We seemed to hit it off. She's sweet and funny and cute. And a great kisser." He picked up the brush and started applying rough strokes to his canvas, maybe getting a bit too aggressive with it.

"Well, what's stopping you from asking her out again?"

"I've gone to the gym every day this week looking for her and she wasn't there. I figured she's probably avoiding me, and I can take a hint."

"Oh, stop boo-hooing and seize the bull by the horns. I'm sure she's not avoiding you. Maybe she's busy. Why don't you put down your paintbrush—since it's doing you no good anyhow—and march on back to the gym and hang out there until you find her. I bet she's going to be thrilled to see you." She plucked the paintbrush from his hand and swatted him on the butt out the door.

"Now, go. And don't come back until you've gotten laid."

If only, Cameron thought. *If only.*

Chapter Eleven

LACY was beat. She'd worked a couple of double shifts at the Mermaid's Purse this week unexpectedly because Meghan had come down with a bad case of strep throat. So, she was working that much more, and she had class and a paper due. She wanted nothing more than to park her butt on the sofa with a tall glass of red wine and something mindless on Netflix. But she felt guilty that she'd not been to the gym all week. Plus she knew she'd benefit far more from a yoga class than from being a couch potato.

So instead of donning a pair of sweats, she pulled on her yoga pants, grabbed her mat, and left for the gym. That glass of wine would have to wait as her reward for good behavior.

As Lacy set up her mat, she glanced around the classroom but was disappointed she didn't see any sign of Cameron. She figured it was a long shot, especially since she'd been out all week, but still. The instructor came in and began the class with everyone on the ground, eyes closed as he talked them through relaxation before they began their practice. She was already glad she'd made the effort to come; something about yoga loosened her mind and body. The only distraction to keep that from happening was the noise from people still filtering into the classroom after it began. She wished they'd lock the door to minimize disturbances, but that was uncharitable, so she pushed the thought aside and began her practice.

By the time Cameron made it to class, he'd missed the beginning relaxation bit, which was a bummer because that always put him in the right mind for the class. Yoga didn't want to come naturally to him; his muscles were tight, and he could never be as limber as some of the women in there who twisted themselves into pretzels for the cause. Sometimes his inability to bend that way made him laugh. Other times, he enjoyed the view, which could be pretty perfect, what with some of the knockout women who attended the class.

Speaking of views, he scanned the classroom, seeing the usual suspects in attendance. There had to be thirty-five or forty people lined up in neat rows throughout the room. He'd never stood at the back before. It gave him a sense of anonymity, so he could better observe without being seen, and it turned out to be perfect. Right there, in the second row from the front, was the object of his obsession: Lacy. In her short shorts, no less. Maybe there was a God after all. Three cheers for dirty laundry.

As the instructor started coaching the class through

Sun Salutations, Cam was filled with anticipation and hoped that wasn't too creepy.

"Inhale and move your right leg back away from your body, with your left foot between your hands. Raise your head." The instructor paced back and forth in the front of the room.

"While exhaling, slide your left foot back and lower it together with your right. Lift your tailbone, keeping your arms straight, and raise your hips while aligning your hands with your arms, hands rooted to the ground."

Which was Cam's cue to look up from his own Downward Dog to catch a glimpse of Lacy's ass in those too-short shorts. He inhaled, but it wasn't because the instructor told him to, but rather because the view took his breath away. In the meantime, he ogled Lacy's butt as he tried to imagine a way they could mix yoga and sex. Distracted, he fell two steps behind the instructor and had to scurry to stand up before the rest of the class started the cycle over again, going back down to the floor.

"Inhale. Raise your torso, extend your arms over your head, and arch your back. Now press your hands to your chest and stand tall, feet together."

Cameron closed his eyes and smiled, happy knowing they had at least five or six more Sun Salutations to go, which meant he'd have plenty of chance to get his fill of the near-perfect scenery in this windowless room.

Cam wasn't gonna lie. Hands down his favorite part of yoga (except for scoping out Lacy) was the final *Shavasana* in which you lie on your back and close your eyes and pretend you're dead. Well, that's not exactly how it worked, but that's how it worked for him, which was a-okay. Laying there without a care in the world for what felt like ten minutes was a little slice of heaven to him, and he always felt restored afterward, like he could take on the world. Too bad it was going to be shot to shit instantly since he'd now have to get up the courage to ask Lacy out.

He was rolling up his mat as he saw her collect her belongings and turn in the direction of the door.

"Hey! Cameron!" She waved and looked happy to see him, which was a good sign. "It's so great to see you here!"

Cam nodded, trying to play it cool. "Lacy! You made it!" D'oh. That was so not cool—it sounded as if he'd been stalking classes looking for her. Which he had, but still.

"Yeah, this ended up being a crazy busy week, so this was the first chance I had to steal away for a while. But I'm glad I did. I always feel so much better afterward."

He nodded. "Ditto for me. You want to grab a quick drink?"

Lacy looked at her watch, which didn't bode well for him if she had to think about it.

Then she waved her hand in the air, dismissing whatever it was she'd been thinking about.

"Yeah, sure," she said. "I could use a drink. Or two."

A ringing endorsement for Cam? Maybe not. But

he'd have to find a way to get her to want him as much as she wanted a drink. It seemed he had his work cut out for him.

Chapter Twelve

SHE hopped into her car and followed Cam to the Dive Bar, a combination dive shop and dive bar that was one of the rare drinking establishments in town primarily patronized by locals. The entrance featured a mannequin dressed in a vintage scuba diver outfit—the type that looked like a primitive astronaut's suit—and served as the de facto doorman. Inside, old fishing nets were draped across the ceiling, and seaweed hung from them like Spanish moss dangling from a live oak tree in Savannah. It was the type of place where you voluntarily ordered a PBR and complained about the lousy tips you got at the restaurant the night before and commiserated with your friends about the traffic the tourists created all over town. It was everything a good local bar should be.

"I love this place so much," Lacy said. "It feels like home every time you step foot in the door."

"I hear ya," Cameron said, bracing himself to own up to his truth. "I don't technically have a home, so it's important to me to have someplace familiar."

"What do you mean don't have a home?"

He sighed as he made air quotes with his fingers. "I'm a starving artist. I was this close"—he held up his thumb and forefinger in measurement—"to landing some steady income when I got my paintings into a local gallery. But then the gallery shut down unexpectedly, and now I'm back to square one. Sorta sucks, but that'll teach me to not become an engineer."

"You don't strike me as the engineering type," Lacy said, reaching for the bowl of party mix the bartender had put on the bar for them.

He lifted his brow. "Is that a good thing or a bad thing?"

She shrugged. "Neither. I mean I've known plenty of engineers in my life, but you seem less, oh, maybe structured than you'd be if you were an engineer."

"I'm an artist. Lack of structure is the hallmark of my existence."

"Like I said." She grinned. "Though it's not like I know a ton about you, you do give off this passionate vibe thing."

"Passionate vibe thing. Hmmm... Sounds like the name of a drink."

She giggled. "I'd have some of that if it was."

"You lacking passion in your life?"

She dipped her head and frowned. "Uh, you did meet the insufferable Billy Crapple, did you not?"

Cameron's text buzzed and he stole a quick glance at it—it was Jamie.

So, are you going back to her place yet?

Cam rolled his eyes, hoping Lacy didn't notice, then quickly typed a reply.

Stop. We're having drinks. Leave me alone.

Jamie sent back a reply with fireworks emojis. He chose to ignore it and turned back to Lacy.

"About that loser ex-boyfriend of yours..."

She held her hands up in defeat. "Don't blame me. It was a huge mistake, one never to be repeated."

"Do you mean Billy Crapple was a mistake? Or what we did in front of Billy Crapple was a huge mistake?"

A flush of red spread across Lacy's face immediately, which Cam found encouraging. If she was annoyed with him, she wouldn't have blushed.

"The mistake was definitely the former, not the latter."

"The latter?" He cocked his eyebrow, intrigued that she couldn't even put words to it.

"Yeah. You know."

He squinted his eyes and glanced at hers. "I know what?"

"I think you enjoyed it as much as I did."

"Why, I haven't the slightest idea of what you're talking about." He pretended to flutter a fan in front of his face to ward off embarrassment.

"Stop joking."

"Trust me, this is no joking matter, Lacy," he said, his face getting serious. "I'm afraid that kiss meant more to me than either of us expected."

She nodded. "I kind of liked it."

He reached over and covered her hand with his on the bar. "That's a gross understatement for me. I kind of haven't stopped thinking about it since it happened."

Her eyes grew wide. "Me too."

He stroked his thumb along hers. "Well, what are we going to do about it?"

She blushed again. "I don't know."

He leaned over and pressed his lips to hers, trying to

restrain himself from wanting to hoist her up onto the bar and have his way with her smack-dab beneath the draping seaweed. "How about a command performance? In someplace a little less obtrusive, perhaps?"

"Such as?"

He pressed his forehead to hers, his breath hitching as he spoke. "I'd invite you back to my place, however, old Mrs. Quimby might die of shock and outrage if she were privy to what might go on." He rapped his knuckles on the bar. "Thin walls."

"Guess that means it's up to me, then?" She arched her brow as his hand settled on her thigh, his finger tracing a figure eight on her skin. She bit her lip. "Well, I do have my own place. And I haven't exactly tested it, but I'm under the impression the walls are fortified to keep the neighbors from minding everyone's business."

"What are we waiting for?" he said, reaching for his wallet and pulling out a twenty. He tossed it on the bar then reached for her hand. "Let's blow this popsicle stand."

Chapter Thirteen

LACY closed her eyes and took a deep breath, employing her yoga relaxation tactics, because this whole thing made her anxious. She hadn't done anything with anyone since she gave that rotten Billy the heave-ho. But Edna's suggestions kept resonating in her head and were empowering her to go for it. Nothing ventured, nothing gained, right?

She was in danger of breaking out in a flop sweat if she didn't get her butt out of the car and into Cam's arms before she chickened out, so she climbed out of her car and motioned with her finger for him to follow her. He quickly exited his car and caught up with her, reaching for her hand.

She lived in a low-rise cedar shake condo a block off the beach. They raced up the wooden walkway that was buffered by protective dunes on either side, climbed a flight of stairs, and she quickly slipped her key into the dead bolt and opened the door.

She barely had both feet in the foyer when Cameron approached her, nuzzling her neck from behind, his hands skating along her sides until they settled on her breasts. Lacy moaned. It had been a lifetime it seemed since she had a man's hands on her there and God, had she missed it. His hands worshipped her breasts, massaging and squeezing them until his fingers found her nipples, already hard.

"Fuck, Lacy," he whispered into her ear as he turned her around to face him. His hands reached the hem of her formfitting tank top, lifting it straight over her head. She stood there in a hot pink workout bra that zipped up the front. "You're killing me." He pretended to plunge a dagger into his heart then quickly tugged the zipper pull and it glided down, allowing her breasts to spill out as soon as the thing separated.

Lacy felt super uncomfortable being the object of his attention. She desperately wanted to squirm as he stood there, not even for a second removing his eyes from her breasts. She had one of those smarmy lines kids said on the playground going through her head: *take a picture; it lasts longer*. But she knew that wasn't exactly the sexiest of comments to make, so she refrained.

Besides, he quickly wrapped his lip around one nipple, and completely hijacked her thoughts. All she could think was that if he kept doing that thing where he alternated his tongue flicking over her nipple and then biting down on it, she was going to climax in about thirty seconds. Though she didn't even have time to let that happen independently before he shimmied her yoga pants down to her ankles, allowing her to step out of them but leaving her standing there in only her panties.

Still sucking her nipple, Cam slipped a hand beneath the leg of her panties and slid his fingers through her slick center on a loud groan.

"Oh, babe, you're so wet, you're killing me." He

pulled his fingers up and lifted them to his mouth, licking and sucking on them as Lacy watched. "You taste even better than I imagined."

Yikes. He imagined what I tasted like? She was so damned out of practice with this stuff. She felt like her body had gone into slow motion, like she was stuck up to her neck in quicksand or something.

He stood before her and touched his fingers to her mouth. "See for yourself." Lacy was willing to believe him and not go there, but he clearly wasn't going to take no for an answer. His other hand had slipped back beneath her panties and *Oh. My. God.* It felt so amazing as his fingers swirled through her moisture and teased her with gentle pressure. He leaned in and licked along Lacy's mouth, his finger between them, and finally Lacy, lost in the sensations of his finger at her swollen center, returned the favor, drawing her tongue along his fingers as his tongue tangled with hers. He drew it across her mouth, coaxing her lips to open to his, where their tongues twined around his slick fingers as her hands scrabbled to push down his boxer briefs and his skimmed her body. That's all it took for Lacy to drop the apprehension and join in the fun, quickly shucking his T-shirt and warm-up pants, no small feat with the tantalizing bulge that had filled out his pants.

Cam wrapped his arms around Lacy, dragging his fingers through her hair with one hand as he pressed her pelvis toward his swollen cock.

"Oh God, I want you so badly," he said, resting his forehead against hers as Lacy's breath came in short pants.

"The feeling's mutual," she said, sliding her hand

along his cock, encircling her fingers around the base and slowly gliding her hand up to the swollen tip as he called her name on a loud moan of pleasure. Lacy dropped to her knees and slid her tongue where her hands had been, trailing around the head as her hands slowly pumped up and down his cock.

"Ahh, Lacy, baby, suck me." He pulled back her hair and watched her. Lacy loved the sound of need in his voice, knowing she could make him feel so desperate for the pleasure she could give him. She opened her mouth wide and slid her lips over the head of his cock and gradually took it into her mouth, adjusting to the size as she flitted her tongue on the top while moving her lips over the head and down the shaft. One hand slid between his legs to fondle his balls while the other kept up the counterbalance to her sucking, sliding up his hard cock as it temporarily slipped from her lips. As she took him deeper into her mouth, she increased the suction, pulling on him while she hummed to create a vibration around his throbbing cock.

She sensed him getting close as he pumped himself in her mouth, but then he stopped, reaching for her.

"Not yet," he said as he pulled her up toward him. "Not without you." He laced his fingers with hers and pulled her into the living room, glancing around then walking her down the hall till they came to her bedroom.

He ushered her through the door as if he was the one who lived there, walking her backward toward the bed. When the back of her knees hit the edge of the bed, he helped to lower her down. "Perfect," he said with a wide grin. "Right where I want you. Now spread your legs for me."

Oh God. Oh God. Oh God. Oh God.

No one had done that to Lacy in about forever. It was certainly not on Billy Crapple's sexual to-do list. But here she was, sprawled across her bed while the hottest guy she'd been around in ages had his hands on her thighs, spreading her legs wide and taking in the view like he was watching his favorite television show.

When she first felt the soft blade of his tongue parting her already slick lips, she gasped from the pleasure of it. She was inclined to close her eyes because, well, it was always a little awkward, no? But when she saw the look of pleasure on his face, she propped herself up on her elbows and took it all in as he worked his mouth on her swollen center, stroking along her lips with his tongue, then circling her clit as he worked his way toward her opening. Gawd, it was crazy how amazing it felt, and she couldn't help but thrust her hips toward his face, glistening with her juices. He slid a finger inside her, and she encouraged him with a long moan as she urged him on with the press of her hips. He reached his other hand to her breasts, fondling and squeezing then plucking her taut nipple. The sensations were overwhelming Lacy, and the throb of lust in her pelvis threatened to overtake her.

"Come for me, Lacy." Cam looked into her eyes as he continued with long, deliberate strokes as her breath came harder and she clutched his head, pressing it toward her. She felt the stirrings coiled deep in her pelvis and suddenly she came alive with intense contractions that radiated throughout her body. She cried out as she pressed herself to his mouth, pleading for more till the tremors subsided.

Cameron scooted up her body till they were face-to-face. His erection pressed into her pussy in a most inviting way.

"Please tell me you have a condom," she said, her eyes pleading.

"I used to be a Boy Scout," he said with a grin, quickly getting up and racing to the foyer, then scurrying back into her room with his wallet, which had been amidst the trail of clothing they'd discarded in haste. He quickly plucked out a telltale foil packet, holding it aloft like a prize.

"'Be prepared,'" she said with a laugh.

He held up three fingers. "Scout's honor." He winked at her.

She pulled him toward her as he settled himself back on the bed, grabbing the package, tearing it open, and impatiently sliding the condom over his hard cock.

"My turn, my little scout friend," Lacy said. She turned to face him and straddled his body, reaching for his cock to position it at her opening as she slid down onto his hard length. They both gasped. Lacy paused for a beat, adjusting to the fullness of him inside her wet warmth, but soon she began to circle her hips, grinding herself against him.

"So good," Cameron said, reaching up to tweak her nipples as she lifted herself slowly off of him and settled back onto him. "So fucking good." He thrust his hips toward her as he grasped her ass and pumped into her. She leaned over, allowing him to pull a nipple into his mouth with a groan. That was all it took for Lacy, who felt her climax building again, only to be hit in wave after wave of pleasure, her pussy greedily clutching his cock.

Cameron rolled over, pinning her beneath him as his hips pumped wildly into her. Lacy wrapped her legs around his hips, linking her ankles to pull him in tighter. Suddenly he stilled, his cock throbbing inside her, as he came, his body jerking as his cock pulsed, till he collapsed on top of Lacy to catch his breath, leaving her to wonder if maybe she'd died and gone to heaven.

Chapter Fourteen

CAMERON wasn't sure if he could get his brain to work for another hour or two, he was so spent. As soon as he had the energy, in what seemed like hours but was more like minutes, he rolled to the side to avoid crushing Lacy.

How'd he have the good fortune to experience earth-shattering sex with the object of his fitness center lust? He must be doing something right.

"Jesus, Cam," Lacy said, still struggling for breath.

He knit his brow as he wiped his wet face, scraping his fingers through her hair. "Everything okay?"

Her eyes grew wide. "Are you kidding? That was, well, crap. I'm trying to come up with a superlative befitting what I experienced under your expert tutelage."

His lips tilted up on one side in a crooked smile. "Damn, I'm glad I lived up to expectations."

"To be honest, I don't know if I even had expectations," she said, blushing. "But whatever I lacked, you made up for, tenfold. No one's done that to me in a long, long time. Like a really long time."

"Made love to you?"

"Well, that too, but the other bit."

He arched a brow. "You mean going down on you?"

She nodded. "That."

"No one has pleasured you with their mouth?"

She sighed. "I had no idea what I was missing out on. It wasn't something Mr. Wonderful would do. He said it was almost like he'd be going down on a guy."

Cam squinted his eyes. "What the fuck does that even mean?"

She nodded. "I know. Right? It's so stupid. But he said since a guy puts his dick in a woman there, then if he puts his mouth there, it's like he's putting his mouth on a guy's dick."

Cameron belted out a laugh. "Wow. That guy's one messed-up dude."

"Which is why I'm not with him."

"Thank goodness."

"Thank goodness indeed. If I was, I'd never know the joys of—"

"Having my tongue on your pussy?"

She breathed in sharply and closed her eyes. "I'm thinking about how amazing it was. You've got one gifted mouth, young man."

"The better to pleasure you with, my dear." He licked his mouth like a wolf and pulled her toward him, tucking her head under his chin as he closed his eyes. "And I'll be glad to return for a command performance as soon as I can recharge my batteries a few."

She curled into him, and they both sighed. "You've got no objections from me." She closed her eyes. "None, whatsoever."

Predawn light slanted through the shades, normally a harsh reminder to Cam that it was time to slip out unnoticed after a one-night stand. Only this didn't feel like a one-off. It felt surprisingly right, like they'd been doing this together for ages. There wasn't the awkward trying to figure each other out, trying to know who liked what and what fit where the best. Granted at first, Lacy seemed a little nervous—if he had a dollar for every time she'd blushed… but in truth, it was quite adorable. Once she set aside her inhibitions, she was as on board as he was, whether it was spreading her legs and sitting on his cock, or later, when she bent herself over the sofa so he could take her from behind.

He was getting hard merely thinking about it. He turned to spoon against her, hoping to get another hour or so of sleep, only to be startled by a phone alarm.

Lacy sat up in bed and glanced at the clock on the wall. "Dammit," she said. "I've got to scramble to get ready for class."

Cam pulled her back down, pressing his front to her back. "Surely that can wait."

She shook her head. "'Fraid not. There are only five people in my class. I would be missed."

He frowned. "You sure about that? Maybe I could write you a school excuse? 'Dear Teacher: Please excuse Lacy Caldwell from class today. She would much rather have a few more orgasms if it's all the same to you.'"

Lacy burst out laughing. "Oh, I'm sure my seventy-year-old professor would totally love that."

Cameron trailed his finger along her belly. "I bet he'd be jealous as hell. And he'd want you to have fun."

She shook her head. "You don't know this guy. He's a misery-loves-company kinda man. He would decidedly not appreciate if I was getting laid and he wasn't."

Cam shrugged. "You never know. Maybe if you don't go to class, and only four people are left, they'll all call in sick today, leaving your professor free so he too can have sex instead of getting up for class."

Lacy lifted the blanket off of her as she climbed out of bed. "As much as I'd dearly love that, I'm afraid it's not even remotely possible. Can I ask for a rain check?"

"Absolutely," he said. "I'm heading out of town for the weekend so let's touch base next week? I'd love a command performance." He stood up and kissed her lightly on the lips. "I'll be counting the minutes."

Chapter Fifteen

LACY'S phone was on silent during class, but it kept buzzing. She couldn't answer it without being rude, so she ignored it. When she had a break, she slipped out to the courtyard to check her messages. Meghan had called four times, Edna two. Shit. What was going on?

She played the first message, from Meghan, and her face went white.

"Listen. It's Vera. I came in for work today and found her slumped over the bar, no pulse, not breathing. I called 9-1-1, I tried to administer CPR, but it was too late. Lacy—Vera died." Meghan's voice burst into tears at that and Lacy tried hard to register what she'd heard. She then played the other five messages, hoping against hope that the first one was wrong. That Vera was fine, she'd only passed out or fallen down, and she was up and moving now. But no. Instead they pleaded with her to please come. As if her rushing there would make a difference now. Shit. How long had she been there, alone, slumped over the bar? Did she have a heart attack? What if Lacy had worked last night? Maybe she'd have stayed past closing and could have saved Vera.

Instead, she was off being selfish, having wild

monkey sex with her fake date. Even though yeah, it didn't seem like such a fake date. It seemed incredibly real and weirdly meaningful, which made no sense since it's not like they knew each other well. Of course it still made her guilty—she shouldn't have gone off and slept with him. Especially if she'd known it was her surrogate mom's last night alive.

Lacy sat on a bench and leaned over, putting her head between her knees. She was woozy, on the verge of passing out. Vera. Gone. Impossible.

After a few minutes, she collected herself and returned to class, politely telling her professor why she had to leave early, and she headed to the Mermaid's Purse, for what would be an incredibly sad day.

The huge neon OPEN sign was dark. That was the first indication that something was terribly wrong. Vera had that place open from ten in the morning till two in the morning, all through high season. She'd cut back the hours a bit in the dead of winter, but mostly it stayed open as much as possible. The Purse was in so many tourist destination books, there were people who traveled to Verity Beach to see the mermaids swimming. So, the Purse was pretty much always open for business. But not today.

Lacy thought there should be some sort of flag hanging at half-mast. The only flag around, however, was a kitschy pirate flag that always flapped on the roof. Who the hell would even know how to get up there to get it down, let alone hang it at half-mast? She smiled. Vera would have said half-assed. She wouldn't want any damned pirate flag hanging half-assed, for sure.

She grabbed a fistful of tissues from a box she kept on her passenger seat and left the car, stopping to wipe more tears from her cheeks as she opened the door.

Inside was eerily silent: no music playing and the sound of sobbing in the distance. How could this have happened? Vera was so young still.

She found Edna and Meghan sitting at the bar, both nursing tumblers of vodka on the rocks. She never drank in the daytime but grabbed the bottle and a glass and poured herself one. They didn't even talk at first. Instead they sobbed and sniffled and cried out loud. At some point, Meghan turned on the television above the bar and clicked to CNN.

"I can't stand to hear us any longer," she said, bursting into tears again.

Edna heaved a sigh, the glass trembling in her aged hands. "That should've been me," she said, blowing her nose.

Meghan and Lacy looked up from their tears, and Lacy put her hand over Edna's. "Don't say that, Edna. It shouldn't have been anyone."

"But I'm an old woman. I've lived my life. It's past my time anyhow."

Lacy looked her firmly in the eye. "That is not the truth. You are the youngest eighty-seven-year-old I've ever met—"

"I'm probably the only eighty-seven-year-old you've

met."

Lacy squinted, thinking that over. "That's possible. But still. You'd better stay with us for a good, long while. You know I'm hiring you to play at my wedding."

"You're getting married? Last I heard you couldn't even get laid."

Meghan spat out her drink. "That might not have been appropriate," she said.

Lacy waved her hand. "No worries. She's right. I couldn't. And I'm not getting married for a long time. I don't even have a boyfriend. But I want you to be here when I do. But—"

"Ahhh…there's a but. Does this have to do with my playing at your wedding? Or about the boyfriend you don't have."

Lacy thrust out her lower lip. "I feel like if I hadn't taken your advice, maybe I'd have been here and saved Vera."

"Wait a minute," she said, holding up a gnarled finger. "You went and hooked up with Romeo?"

"Since when do eighty-seven-year-olds use terms like hooked up?" Lacy sighed. "And yes, I did hook up with him. But now I feel awful about it. I was having fun while my surrogate mama was taking her last breaths."

"Look, Lace," Meghan said, putting her arm around her friend. "Don't leap to conclusions. We don't even know the time she died or how she died. Chances are likely no one could have saved her, even if they were sitting right here when it happened, whatever it was. So, stop beating yourself up. And maybe you can share details of your hookup so we can get our minds off of our sadness."

Lacy looked at Meghan and Edna. "Is that appropriate when you're in mourning to discuss such things?"

"If I had a handbook, I'd look it up, but I don't because there isn't one," Edna said. "You're amongst good friends and we'd like to be distracted, so spill. And spare us no details." Meghan looked at Edna, her mouth agape, shocked at her bluntness.

"All right, all right. Fine." Lacy held her hands out to keep the peace. "I went to yoga and then we went for drinks and came back to my place and he's really, really, really good at, like, the things that matter most."

"He went down on you?" Meghan clapped her hands. "Yay, Lacy. Your dry spell is officially wet." She smiled through a veil of tears. "Vera would be so happy for you."

"Can I say congratulations for seizing the moment and accosting that young man?"

"I didn't accost him!"

"Well, you had pledged to be aggressive, and while that works with some, it doesn't with others, so I'm glad it was the right tack with him."

"I don't think anywhere in my wording did I say I was going to be aggressive. I simply took your words to heart."

"I think the next question on everyone's mind, then, is…" Edna held up her hands as if measuring the distance between her two palms.

Lacy lifted a brow. "You two do know we're here in shock, mourning the loss of our dear friend. And you're talking about penis sizes."

"Distractions. We need distractions." Edna pulled a

cigarette from her purse and stuck it in her mouth.

"You can't smoke that in here," Lacy said. "It's against the law."

"I'm going to pretend I'm smoking. I'm stressed. It's what I do when I'm stressed. Tell us about him."

"You mean about how endowed he is? Or about him?"

"I'm being serious. Tell us about him."

"He's handsome and has the most amazing blue eyes. He's sweet and thoughtful. And interesting. And he doesn't spend all the time talking about himself like idiot used to. I like him."

"Well, I hope you like him, considering you had his cock in your mouth."

It was Lacy's turn to spit out her drink. "Edna! What are you saying?"

She waved her hand, her unlit cigarette between her fingers. "Good God, woman. Do you think I fell off a turnip truck? If you didn't do that then I'd have to ask you why."

"I'm not sure I'm comfortable with this line of questioning."

"Which is why I'm not questioning, I'm filling in the blanks for you. You used protection, I hope?"

"Hell, yeah, I used protection."

"So, when are you going to hook up again?" Edna refilled her vodka and took a pretend drag from her smoke.

"I have no idea. I mean, sometime? I'm kind of swamped. Plus, with this, who knows what is going to happen."

Meghan's eyes opened wide. "What do you mean?"

Lacy shrugged. "Does anyone know what the Plan B for this place would be?" She opened her arms and motioned toward the rest of the restaurant. "Edna, you worked with her the longest. Any idea?"

Edna shook her head. "We never talked about dying. That wasn't in the plans."

"Well, shit," Lacy said. "We have no idea if we're all going to be out of a job?"

"I can't imagine anyone would close this place down. It's iconic. They'd be crazy to do that."

But Lacy knew crazier things could happen. She'd just experienced one such event. She made a mental note to find out what relatives Vera had around town to see if any of them knew what would become of the Mermaid's Purse.

Chapter Sixteen

CAM had spent several days in Virginia with his father, whose decline from Alzheimer's was becoming scarier by the day. Twice he'd slipped away from the nursing home. Once he showed up in the woods behind the building; the other time he wandered down a side street in his bare feet and pajamas. It had taken every last penny remaining in his dad's coffers to put his father in this facility, and it plucked Cam's last nerve they couldn't even keep him contained. The fact was, his father was too far gone to remain at home: he wasn't safe. Sooner or later he was going to accidentally light the house on fire or drink cleaning fluid. It was like having an elderly toddler who could, in fact, overpower you if you made him mad or told him the truth or even told him lies, for that matter. Cam felt horrible condemning him to his final days or months or years in an institution. But he couldn't deal with him on his own, and his selfish brother was of no use with either his time or his money.

So there his father sat, plopped in front of the television, staring into oblivion, except when he got ornery, which was happening more and more often. When that did occur, they occasionally had to subdue him. Cam wanted to make sure he wasn't around if and when that happened. He was never too keen on his old man. As a navy captain, his father was used to giving orders and enforcing rigid restrictions, and he doled them out generously. He was incapable of complimenting Cam, and with that ultimatum about his professional choices, well, in many ways Cam had given up on his dad anyhow. He thought it was downright generous of him to have put him in this facility rather than leaving him in Depends undergarments in a backyard tent and hoping for the best.

At last, Cam was out of there, after four arduous days hanging out with his dad. He'd run out of conversation, which hardly mattered because the old man looked at him as if he were a stranger who had broken into his home, with little to tie the two men together except for some shared DNA. It was heartbreaking, and Cam hoped one day not to repeat the mistakes of his father with his own children. Not that children were on any horizon of his. Hell no. Although he was starting to think how much fun it would be to practice making babies with Lacy Caldwell. Don't they say it's all about the journey anyhow? He could pave the road to parenthood with some kick-ass sex, and simply thinking about the many ways made his cock stiffen in his pants.

Thank goodness, he was on the highway and not sitting in a nursing home with an erection. That would have been cause for concern. Explain that one to the staff. About his staff. Ha. He laughed at his dumb joke.

He'd realized too late that he hadn't gotten contact information for Lacy after their little tête-à-tête. At least he knew where she lived, though he wasn't necessarily comfortable showing up at her place unannounced yet, either. He could figure out a way to get hold of her, or at least wait to find her at the gym, but he wished he could call her right now. Tell her how sad he felt after spending a depressingly long half of a week with his dad. Even if he and his old man didn't get along well, it was tragic to see a once strong, vibrant, and unfortunately overly macho man reduced to a blank stare and shitting his pants. There was no dignity in aging, was there?

He had no one to call but Jamie and she hadn't answered his earlier call, nor had she bothered to call back, so he checked his voicemail in case Lacy had tracked him down. No such luck. But there was one message on there.

"This is Charles Fourney. I'm an estate attorney in Verity Beach. I have a client who passed away recently and has left something to you."

A client left him something? Was it going to be a leg lamp? Or a velvet Elvis, maybe? He knew one thing: it wasn't going to be something of value. Why even bother returning the call? But by the time he returned to his rental room, he'd received another call.

"Mr. Sanders, I was hoping we could meet sometime this week to discuss your inheritance."

"My inheritance? Sounds cryptic. Particularly because I don't know anyone who died recently."

"Then this must be your lucky day because some lovely woman who happens to be my client remembered you in her will. Would you meet me in my office at nine?"

Cameron shrugged. Not as if he had any particularly important things to do slated on his schedule. What the hell? Nothing ventured, nothing gained.

"Great Aunt Vera?" Cam stared openmouthed at an older, gray-haired gentleman, who sat across from him at an expensive mahogany desk. The man smiled kindly as he rifled through a huge stack of papers and started to explain what this whole thing was about.

"Seriously, I'm afraid there's been some mistake. I haven't the slightest idea who—or what—you're talking about."

"I'm telling you. My client had no other immediate relatives. Apparently your mother was a second cousin to her? She met you when you were a small child at a family reunion, and she took a liking to you. It was at that point that she wrote you in as the heir to her business."

"What do you mean, her business?"

"She's the owner of a bar, the one with mermaids. You must know about it—the one off the highway, down near the beach?"

"Yeah, of course. The one all the tourists go to." He scratched his head. "That was owned by someone I was related to?"

"Evidently. And she never married. She said her immediate family looked down on her for having the bar and restaurant, so she'd show them by leaving it to someone else. And that someone else is you.

Additionally her request was that the will be filed immediately upon her death, so we can get the ball rolling on this, get it through probate so that you can take over the property as soon as possible."

Cameron shook his head, unable to process this information. Someone he didn't even know left him her most valuable possession. How weird was that? And what on earth was he going to do with it? Run it? He didn't know anything about running a bar. Particularly one with a damned mermaid pool attached. Sounded like a huge money pit.

"We can go over details as this moves through the legal system. We'll pay off outstanding debt, which won't amount to much but monthly bills since Vera ran a tight show. I expect no problems with it and it should be all settled within a few months' time."

"And then what?"

"And then you're the proud owner of a famous roadside attraction that draws tourists from far and wide."

"In the meantime, who's going to keep it going, so it doesn't run into the ground?"

"Vera made allowances in here for you to run it prior to finalizing the inheritance. For the time being the staff is trying to juggle things, but we'll give you a few days to sleep on it and figure things out and then I can set you up for a tour of the place."

Well, hell. Going from essentially jobless to being shackled to some godforsaken tiki lounge in the blink of an eye. If that didn't take the damned cake. Sleep on it, indeed. For that matter, he was more likely gonna need to get drunk on it. This was an awful lot to swallow.

Chapter Seventeen

LACY seemed to float around in a gray haze of sadness in the week since Vera's passing. The funeral was a beautiful service, but it certainly didn't bring closure, what with the suddenness of her death. No one knew what was going to happen with the Mermaid's Purse Tiki Bar and Lounge. There were rumors afoot that she'd left it to some random guy, but no one knew who he was or what he planned to do with the place. Lacy no longer knew she could count on an income from the job—maybe this guy would fire everyone and bring in his own staff? It would be bad enough being jobless, but then to also have the many friendships fostered at the Purse essentially severed would be even harder to stomach.

All of this added up to leaving Lacy sad, stressed, and surly. She knew the best course of action would be to go back to the gym, get those endorphins flowing, maybe chill the hell out in yoga. But she didn't have the time. She was busy pitching in with everyone else to keep the place afloat for the time being. Plus she was plunged into midterm exams. She was a bit bummed she hadn't heard boo from Cam, but maybe it was better that way. She'd had her needs met—temporarily, at least—and now she needed to face the real world, which was one involving potential unemployment with tuition bills and rent to pay. She didn't have time to deal with a guy, even if he was extremely handsome and sweet and amazing in the sack. She had an all-nighter ahead of her tonight to prepare for a big exam in the morning, so she knew where her focus needed to be.

"Wait a second," Jamie said. "Let me get this straight. You didn't even know this woman and she left you the mermaid bar? That's freaking awesome."

"Awesome?" Cam said as he pulled into a parking spot at the Piggly Wiggly supermarket. "What the hell am I going to do with a bar?"

"I can think of plenty of things. For example, drink."

He laughed. "I can drink without having to own a bar. That's like saying you need to be a fireman to have a fire in the fireplace."

"Bad analogy but whatever. Just sayin' I'd be totally digging it if I were you. So, when are you taking me?"

"I haven't even been there myself."

"Are you kidding me? You've been sitting on this news for days and you didn't tell me, and meantime you didn't go in there and tell everyone they better suck up to you or they're canned?"

"Uh, no, I did not fire anyone. Nor did I threaten to. I've been ruminating."

"Honestly, Cam. You are the only person I know who could be without a job for all intents and purposes and complain when a job drops in your lap."

"But the job I want is to be an artist. One who makes a living that way, not a starving artist."

"And, voila. Here you go—this is the golden ticket to afford you the opportunity to earn money plus paint on the side. You'll have something steady to keep food on the table. But actually, wait a minute—this place is a restaurant, too, right? So now you get free meals and booze. Damn, Cam. How much luckier could you get?"

He felt like if it included Lacy, it would be even better. Shame that wasn't a negotiation option. He grabbed two grocery bags from the back of the car and made his way into the store for the staples: milk, bread, cereal, juice. He wasn't one to fix elaborate meals anyhow, but with his living situation, cooking anything other than what could fit in a toaster oven wasn't an option. That or boiled in an electric kettle. If he was feeling wild, he'd fix up some hard-boiled eggs, but today he wasn't up for the added effort.

"Let's go tonight! I want to check this place out. I haven't been there in years. One of those funny things— you live here and don't even think to go there, yet people come from thousands of miles away to see it."

"Am I supposed to announce myself as the new slumlord?"

"No. Definitely not. Let's go check I out. It'll be fun!"

"Whoa, dude, this place is rockin'," Jamie said as they walked into the place. If you don't want it, I do."

"I don't know what I want, James. This all seems weird to me. Me, a proprietor of a drinking establishment."

"Right? Lucky you!"

Cam shook his head. She didn't get it.

He'd been pouting around for days feeling super bummed he'd not seen Lacy at the gym. He assumed he'd have seen her since the last time, which had been lingering in his brain so much. Maybe she wasn't as into it as he was. She did sort of kick him out that morning. It had left him feeling grumpy and out of sorts. And maybe a little ungrateful for this gift that had dropped into his lap out of nowhere. But still—spend the rest of his life running a bar? Nooo thank you, ma'am.

They walked through the lounge, past the dining room, and into the bowels of the bar where the lights were dim. In front of them, almost like an oversized portrait perched behind the bar, was a huge window that led your eyes into a watery world.

"So weird," Cam said. "What bar has water behind it?"

"One that has mermaids in the water," Jamie said, pointing at a beautiful swimming mermaid who suddenly appeared right before them doing loops and twirls in the water as gracefully as a ballerina. This mermaid was wearing a melon-orange tail, and her long blond hair floated around her like an ethereal crown of seagrasses. Cam had never seen something so weird and sexy and downright odd. It made him think for a minute that mermaids did indeed exist until he shook his head and remembered they were in a tiki lounge and that was some plain old woman wearing a tail suit.

"The coconut tits are a nice touch," Jamie said, pointing at her bikini top.

He shrugged. "Beach theme, it works."

They found two seats at the bar and glanced at the drink menu.

"Oooh," she said, running her finger down the list, which included pictures of each drink. "I can't decide between Sex with the Captain or something a little more mermaidy."

"Sex with the Captain?" Cam lifted an eyebrow.

She giggled. "Right? It's got Captain Morgan's spiced rum, of course, but the rest of it sounds like a hot mess: amaretto almond liqueur, peach schnapps, cranberry and orange juice. I'll take a pass. Imagine how bad that would be puking it up."

"The Tipsy Dolphin looks pretty—nice and bright pink. It's got vodka, raspberry lemonade, ginger ale, and cranberry juice."

"Yeah, it's pretty, but I'm not a pink drink girl. Yum—the Purple Flip-Flop looks good. It's made with pomegranate juice, pineapple juice, coconut rum, and vodka. It's such a pretty shade of purple!"

"Maybe I'll get whatever's on tap and be done with it."

"I'm telling you, Cam"—she pointed at the menu—"with your glum, shipwreck of an attitude lately, you'd better go with the Gilligan's Island. But ugh, it's got peach schnapps, too. On second thought, probably what you'd be better off with is a Creamy Sex on the Beach."

"Tell me about it." He rolled his eyes.

"Tell you about what?" She cocked her head toward him.

"No doubt I'd be better off with a Creamy Sex on the Beach, being that I can't get my own creamy sex on the beach."

"For the record, I said 'a,' not 'some.' Far be it from me to dare suggest again you go find that girl and do the nasty."

He shook his head. "Newsflash, J. I did. And we did." He stuck his lower lip out.

Her eyes opened wide. "You did? And?"

"Annnnd, I'm sitting at a bar with you, not her. Capiche?"

"Well, what'd you do—scare her off with that big dick of yours?"

He wrinkled his brow. "I'm pretty sure she had as much fun as I did, judging by the sounds she made and the many times she called my name. But since then, crickets."

"Well, did you call her?"

He shook his head. "I forgot to get her number."

She frowned. "Sometimes I worry you are romantically stunted, my friend. You need to put on your damned detective hat and go find her for God's sake. It's a small town—she can't have gone far."

"But if she wanted me, she'd have found me."

Maybe she's pissed that you didn't call her. I would be if I were her."

"You think?"

"I know. If a girl sleeps with you then she wants you to make the first move. She doesn't want to seem needy or clingy."

"That's stupid."

"Tell that to your idiotic sex. They're the ones who made that a bad thing to begin with."

"I dunno, James. I mean, it's weird now. Time has elapsed and it seems like the window of opportunity has closed on things."

"No, actually, it sounds like you chose to close the window yourself without even trying." She hit her fist on his head. "Now that I think of it, you definitely need the Creamy Sex on the Beach to get your mind off of the creamy sex on the beach you're not having. It sure sounds yummy—vodka, coconut rum, pineapple juice, grenadine, heavy cream. Oh, but there is that damned peach schnapps again. I hate that stuff. It's like the worst cough syrup ever invented."

They ordered their drinks then toasted when the bartender, a sixty-something woman with tat-sleeved arms, delivered them.

"Here's to being the brand spanking new owner of a mermaid tiki bar, my friend," Jamie said as she clinked glasses with him. "I'll be here nightly for my free drink allotment."

The bartender seemed to turn to say something to them but appeared to change her mind and busied herself with wiping down the bar.

"Don't count your chickens on that," Cam said,

taking a sip of his drink. "That's pretty damned good." He licked his lips. "I don't know what I'm doing yet."

"Why don't you sell this place if it's so odious to you to run it? If a free damned bar and restaurant is going to be such a burden, then sell the place to a developer so he can plunk down some fancy condos. I bet this property is worth a fortune."

"Huh," Cam said. "I hadn't even thought about that. Shit, that is a brilliant idea. Cash out and my financial troubles would be over and done with."

"I mean, it would be sad to see an institution like this disappear, but that's progress, right?" Jamie took a swig of her drink. "I wish I'd had some Creamy Sex on the Beach, too. Waaaaa." She rubbed her fisted hands over her eyes like a bawling baby."

"Whassa matter? Baby Jamie need to get laid?" Cameron laughed as he gave her a sip of his drink.

She stopped fake crying. "Hell no, honey. I'm perfectly happy juggling two surfer dudes right now and am having more than enough sex these days, thanks. But I think I will order one of those because they're mighty tasty."

"Wait a minute, you're a veritable manwhore in women's clothing. You're sleeping with two guys at once?"

She nodded. "Yep. It's all perfectly aboveboard. I've cleared it with both of them and they're more than happy to be commitment-free, so all good."

"Seriously, sometimes I wonder if you're a man in disguise."

"Trust me, watching all the crapola going on with my warring parents, the last thing on my mind is a relationship with a man where I'd have to slice open my wrists and bleed for him. I'm happy with a little on the side for now, minus the drama."

"Yet here I am, the one blubbering about a girl. Maybe we need to do some Freaky Friday thing and do a personality switch so we match better."

"Maybe you need another Creamy Sex on the Beach so you can grow a set and then go find your own creamy sex on the beach."

"If you're buying."

"But when we leave here I'm going to make you go find her and do the deed, so you'll stop with the hangdog face."

"What? You're going to make me go to her place?"

"You know where she lives?"

He wrinkled his brow. "Of course I do. That's where we did it. You didn't think I was going to bring her to my hovel, did you?"

"Bartender, can I have another of these," she pointed to his drink. "For him?" She pointed at Cam.

"You drink up at your new bar, honey. I'll be the designated driver, so you don't have to."

Chapter Eighteen

LACY'S nose was buried in a textbook when her phone rang.

"Lace, it's me, Juno."

"Hey, everything going okay at the Purse?"

"Look, I've got important information I overheard, and I wanted you to know about it."

Lacy sat up straight. "What?"

"A couple came into the bar tonight and were chatting and next thing you know I overheard her telling him he should sell this place to a developer and he agreed. He said it would solve all his financial problems, and she said it would be a shame to see it go, but that's progress."

"Ohhh, shit. That's not good. Not good at all." Lacy took in a deep breath and sighed loudly. "You're sure that's what you heard?"

"As sure as the scene on the wild west that is tattooed up my left arm."

There was indeed such a scene, complete with gunslingers and cowboys and Indians on horseback.

"Thanks for letting me know, Juno. Please relay this to Edna and Meghan and the rest of the staff. We have to figure out what we're going to do. We have to save the Mermaid's Purse from some greedy rat bastard who wants to destroy everything Vera worked her whole life to build."

She stood up and paced the living room, staring out at the dark night sky and the even darker ocean beyond it. Crap. How can it be that in the blink of an eye everything Vera had created could be destroyed? That was so wrong. There must be something they could do to save the tiki bar.

"You doing okay, Cammy boy?" Jamie asked as she shut the door, put the key in the ignition, then backed out onto the road. "Tell me where I'm turning off so I can see where your girlfriend-who's-not-your-girlfriend lives. I promise I won't TP her house or set a bag of dog poop on fire at her doorstep. I'm curious to see where she lives."

"Maybe I shouldn't have had that fourth drink," Cameron said. "I thought I could handle my liquor, but those were some strong drinks."

"Right? At your fancy schmancy new restaurant. And once you're running it, you can put less alcohol in them, and that will save you money too!"

"I don't want to talk about that right now. I have to tell the lawyer in the next few days what I'm going to do with the place."

"Fair enough. I think you'll be able to wait for your

upcoming hangover to subside before you have to make any irrevocable decisions."

"Turn down here," he said with a slight a drunken slur, pointing his right hand out the window. "Then make a left and you'll see it." He waved his hand. "There— that's her place. On the second floor."

"Let's get out and walk closer so I can have a better view."

"Nah, I'm good."

"But I'd like to. Come on." She unhitched her seatbelt and got out, and Cameron followed as she opened the door for him. "Let's go check it out." She grabbed his hand and pulled him out.

"See. It's there." He pointed yet again at Lacy's building.

"Cool. It's really nice." She turned and ran back to her car, hopped in, and promptly locked the doors. She put her window down. "Okay, Ace, I'm counting on you to not fuck this up, got it? Let me know how it goes!"

And she drove away, leaving Cam standing on the walkway to Lacy's condo at midnight, drunk and tired as shit.

Who the hell would be knocking quietly on her door at midnight on a Tuesday, Lacy wondered as she stood on tiptoes to peer through the peephole. Well, damn. Of all the things, he was about the last person she'd expect to show up at this point. She opened the door and ushered him in, still a bit ticked that he didn't have the decency to reach out to her after the last time they were together.

"Cameron," she said, her voice stiff. She gave a polite nod and deliberately made no body contact with him.

"Lacy." Cameron stood before her in a pair of khaki shorts and a wrinkled red-and-white-ticking button-down with a stain on the front of it.

"Did you, uh, forget something?" She frowned. "Besides your manners, that is."

He stood there, blinking as if he was trying to recall something. He smelled strongly of coconut rum, of all things. "Crap, Lacy. It's been a weird time of it lately. I'm sorry if you think I've been a dick for not calling you. Except in my defense, I didn't have your number."

She glanced at her watch, placed her hands on her hips, and sighed. "Look, Cameron. It's late. You look like you've been through the wringer. I've got a lot of studying to do. I'm totally cool if you didn't want to get together again. It's fine. But seriously, I've got a super busy day tomorrow, and I've had a hard week. I'm not in the frame of mind for any bullshit excuse making, okay?"

"I'm not here for excuse making."

"Well, then why are you here?"

He squinted. "Do you want to know the truth?"

"That's generally a good place to start."

"Because Jamie tricked me."

Lacy nodded her head. "Ah. I see. Of course. Jamie. Jamie tricked you." She walked toward the door and reached for the handle. "Now, if I can see you out?"

He held up his hands. "No, wait. Hear me out." He

eyed the sofa with a sad sort of longing. Lacy didn't want him to get comfortable because then it would only be that much harder to evict him, but she, too, was uncomfortable standing in the foyer.

"Fine. Have a seat." She walked over to the couch and sat on the far side of it, well out of his reach.

"Just don't light any matches because I think the alcohol on your breath might catch the place on fire."

"Do you know before we got together—" He paused. "It's okay to say we got together, right? It's not like I'm saying, 'before we hooked up,' which sounds a bit more tawdry."

She nodded, even though at this point, it was purely a hookup. But whatever. That's what she intended going into it, so why split hairs when she got what she came for. And came. And came. And came. Ugh, the thought of that settled deep in her pelvis and made her want to squirm from the memories. The man had a talented tongue and knew how to use it.

"Before we got together, but after we first kissed, I was so obsessed with you that I couldn't even paint. All I could think of was that kiss. And all I could paint were vaginas."

Lacy knit her brows. "Um, what?"

He waved his hands as if to erase that comment. "That didn't come out right. My point was I couldn't paint, I was stuck, I kept thinking of you and how badly I wanted to see where that kiss would lead. Except I knew it wasn't real on your part."

Lacy crossed and uncrossed her legs, trying to get more comfortable since this conversation was taking on a life of its own. "How do you know it wasn't real on my part?"

"You said yourself that you needed someone to be a fake date to show your ex."

"Yeah, and you agreed to be a fake date. So as far as I knew, you had no interest in me beyond being polite and sticking to your assigned role that day."

"Except that I honestly liked that kiss. A lot. I wished it had been real."

"Well, me too. But I knew it wasn't."

"Except that it was." He turned to her. "I think I jacked off thinking about you and that kiss at least twice a day for a week afterward."

"You did?" Lacy didn't know whether to be flattered or weirded out. "Because?"

He combed his fingers through his hair. "Because I wanted to be with you so badly. But I assumed you didn't want to be with me."

"Well, that was presumptuous of you."

"You mean you did?"

"Um, I was, wasn't I? Or was that my imagination, what happened between us. And who is this guy Jamie?"

"It's Jamie's fault I found you that night at yoga class." He scratched his chin. "I was too chicken to approach you, but she berated me until I agreed to do something. She pretty much lit the match under my ass to act on my feelings."

"So that explains your showing up at yoga and us going out for drinks."

"And then—"

"And then. But why are you here now?"

"I missed you, but I didn't know how to get ahold of you. And I've had a hard week and I didn't know what to do."

"Um, you did know where I lived."

"Yeah, but you didn't reach out to me, so I figured maybe you weren't all that interested."

"We made love repeatedly over the course of like ten hours. Generally speaking I don't do that if I'm not interested."

"How was I supposed to know?"

"Oh, maybe because I shared my body with you?"

"Why didn't you get in touch with me then?"

"I had less of a way to find you than vice versa. Plus it's been a super bad couple of weeks. I lost a dear, dear friend and was thrown for a loop by that. I've been up to my eyeballs in work. I could barely keep on top of things, let alone hunt down some guy who couldn't be bothered reaching out to me."

She didn't want to get into the details about losing Vera. She hadn't shared with Cam about her mermaid gig in the first place since she was too embarrassed to let him know that's how she paid her bills. She figured he'd think it was silly, frivolous, or too strange.

"Weird, all these people dying."

"Huh? Who else?"

"What?" he knit his brows. "Nothing. Disregard that."

"So… You still haven't told me why you came here tonight."

His eyes were looking drowsy, his lids draping down over them like Fourth of July bunting on a wraparound porch. "Ahh, yes, Jamie."

"So, about this Jamie guy."

"Girl."

"Huh?"

"Jamie. Jamie's a girl. Well, make that a woman. Although I don't think of her like that."

"What do you think of her as?"

"She's a good friend."

Lacy nodded. "You mean she's not a girlfriend, then?"

He held his hands up. "Oh God, no. We'd kill each other if we ever tried that."

"So, what does she have to do with you being here?"

He blinked slowly. She half expected him to plunk over sound asleep on the sofa.

"We had a few drinks. She tricked me into showing her where you live. Then she tricked me into getting out of the car. Then she got back in and drove away."

Lacy burst out laughing. "With friends like that, who needs enemies?"

"Which is what I'm going to tell her when I get ahold of her." He turned toward her on the sofa, resting his head sideways on the cushion as he extended his legs onto the furniture as well.

"You don't have a car here, do you?"

He shook his head.

"Just as well because I wouldn't let you drive anyhow." She stood up. "Okay, fine. You can stay here but on the sofa. I'll grab you a blanket and a pillow and please, if you'd remove your shoes that would be good."

He nodded, kicked off his shoes, then curled up in a ball on her couch, resting his head on his folded hands.

When she returned with the blanket and pillow, he was sound asleep, and all she could hear was the quiet chuff of his breath.

Chapter Nineteen

CAM woke before dawn with a raging headache and a throbbing woody. Or would that be a throbbing headache and a raging woody? Who knew? But he had a desperate need to take care of both, so he dragged himself off the sofa and padded down the hall to the bathroom, where he rifled beneath the sink till he found a bottle of Advil.

He peed, but that did little to improve things down there. Probably because the minute he realized where he was, all he could think of—besides the throbbing in his brain—was how much he wanted a command performance of the last time. Clearly he'd fumbled that effort last night. He saw some toothpaste on the sink and squeezed a strip onto his finger, then proceeded to finger brush his stale liquor mouth, hoping to be at the ready in case the opportunity presented itself.

As he left the bathroom, he paused outside her bedroom, where the door was cracked. He swore he heard some weird humming sound emanating from there, but he couldn't quite determine what it was. He stood as close to the door as possible without nudging it and tried to glimpse into her room to see if everything was okay.

He heard a few soft groans from her and it worried

him. What if something was really wrong and he was right there and did nothing to help her? He'd never forgive himself. But what if she was asleep, and who knows what that sound was? Maybe it was coming from downstairs, or upstairs.

He finally made the executive decision to enter the room when he heard her groan yet again. "Is everything okay?" His eyes struggled to adjust to the darkness, but soon he could make out Lacy. A very naked Lacy. On top of her comforter. Her legs spread wide. A vibrator in her hand. *Holy fuck.*

This was like a fantasy come to life, waking to a woman in a nearby room pleasuring herself. Where the person having the dream suddenly becomes part of the dream. And boy, had he had this dream many a time in his life. He could not stop staring at her as she slowly guided the small vibrator along her wet pussy, occasionally moving it to stimulate a nipple, but then returning to her slickness, then gradually inserting it inside herself.

Jesus, it was as if Cam had died and gone to heaven. He looked down to his boxer shorts and that morning hard-on had taken on epic proportions. He could've hosted a two hundred-person wedding beneath that tent.

Meanwhile, had she not seen him? Was she so engrossed in her own pleasure, chasing an orgasm like she was, that she didn't even notice him?

She moaned and he couldn't help but gasp as he reached for his hard cock, pumping his hand along the length, coaxing it to come even more alive.

Lacy opened her eyes and looked up at him. "It's about time you came in here, you idiot."

His eyes widened. Seriously? She wanted him here? This was a trap—in the best possible way.

"Come," she said, patting the space on the bed beside her.

"You need to come first," he said, smiling. Funny how horniness could do away with a blazing headache in no time flat.

"Oh, believe me, I intend to." She continued to glide the small blue vibrator along her lips, around her clit, then back again, sometimes pressing it deep inside. Then she held up the device. "Would you like to do the honors?"

Jesus, Mary, and Joseph, was this real? There was every chance in the world this was all some weird dream he was having. Because how could it be real? Hell to the yeah, he wanted to do the honors.

He grabbed the vibrator and dragged his tongue along the length of it before returning to echo the same path Lacy had traced along her center, which was drenched now with her juices. He leaned over and opened his mouth to one of her nipples, enveloping the areola in his mouth and sucking hard as his tongue flicked the tip. Lacy spread her legs wider and bent her knees. Cam took advantage of the invitation and shifted his body downward till he centered himself between her legs. He slid the vibrator deep into her pussy while his tongue worked its magic along her lips and clit.

"Oh, fuck, Cam, that's incredible." Lacy thrust her hips toward him, tiny moans of pleasure escaping her lips repeatedly.

"I want you to come all over my mouth, Lace." He inserted a finger into her center, holding the vibrator up against her G-spot as his tongue lapped greedily at her wetness. Lacy let out a loud groan and fell apart, her body thrashing as he held his mouth tight to her pussy, sucking her juices until she pushed his mouth away.

"I'm guessing you don't have any condoms lying around?" Cam had failed to replace the two he'd used from his wallet, and they'd searched everywhere for the old one she'd found in a nightstand drawer when they'd gone for round three.

Lacy pulled him toward her. "Get here. Now." She encircled his length with her hand and stroked him, slowly at first but increasing the speed. "I'm clean if you're clean. And I've been on the pill forever. I want you here, now." She pointed toward her pelvis.

He needed no other encouragement and spread her legs with his knees as he settled between her legs, notching the tip of his cock to her wet opening and happily sliding himself into her warm, wet body. He sighed with pleasure and stayed seated in her for a few beats, enjoying the sensation. Soon he began to slowly pull out and press back in as she thrust her hips to his, rubbing her clit against him. Their movements became frenzied as both climbed toward climax, with Cam pumping his cock into her, desperate to satiate his need to orgasm. At last, he felt the boulder barreling down the hill and he stiffened, planted deep inside her as wave after wave of his seed spurted into Lacy. Seconds later, she followed him over the edge, her pussy squeezing his cock till they both lay spent, gasping for air.

"Good God, you know how to turn a man on," he said after he caught his breath. She was pressed against his chest as he stroked her hair. "That was spectacular."

"You didn't think I was going to kick you out of my condo without a little makeup sex, now, did you?"

He chuckled. "To be honest, I assumed I was dead in the water."

She wrapped her arms around him as her tongue swiped his lips, angling to deepen the kiss. "The fact is, I've grown quite fond of you, Cameron Sanders."

"The feeling is mutual, Lacy Caldwell. The feeling is quite mutual."

Chapter Twenty

THE next several days were a whirlwind for Lacy between exams and work. She'd finally given Cameron her phone number but warned him she'd be impossible to reach. Arriving for her late shift at the bar, she'd donned her favorite mermaid tail tonight—a sparkly silver number with an ethereal pink trail of fabric coming from the end of the tail. She had on her pearl-encrusted bikini top, secured with beaded pearl straps, and her hair was side-braided again.

She put on her goggles and plunged into the pool, proceeding with a routine of twists and turns and flips for the customers to watch while they drank and ate dinner. She and Emily, another one of the mermaids who had a mass of titian curls that cascaded from her shoulders, danced through the water as if synchronized in their movements. Emily was wearing a green tail, which showed off her hair so nicely. When Emily was working, no one ever seemed to notice Lacy, which didn't bother her in the least. As long as they shared tips, it was all good.

The two of them played around in the water, flapping tails and circling figure eights around one another. Lacy loved coming to work here—she was able to set her cares poolside when she dove into the water and swimming in a mermaid tail was meditative to her. Sometimes she fantasized what it would truly be like to be a mermaid in the ocean. But she was happy she was in a climate-controlled body of water, with no creepy things floating around, and she could remove her tail and have amazing sex that involved spreading her legs and wrapping them around a certain man's hips just so. It was all she could think about, and she'd texted Cam in case he was interested in a late-night visit after her shift at the bar, but she hadn't heard back from him yet.

It was a light night with fewer patrons—Mondays usually were—so there were only a handful of people at the bar at any given time. Which was why she noticed when a man with dark, wavy hair and strikingly blue eyes came up to the bar and pulled up a barstool. Cameron. Crap. What was he doing here? And would he recognize her? Maybe not. After all, it wasn't as if he'd ever seen her in a mermaid's tail before. Plus her hair was braided down her side—she'd never worn it like that for him. She had a pair of goggles obscuring her eyes. No way would he recognize her. Fact was, there wasn't much she could do at this point anyhow. She had to work this shift, she needed the money, and this is what the patrons of the Mermaid's Purse were expecting: two mermaids floating through the water.

She tried to let Emily be front and center as much as possible—men were so attracted to her hair that they always paid more attention to her. Not as if she wanted Cam to be turned on by her, though. But still. She only hoped he was gone before her shift ended at eleven.

She'd set up discussions with the employees at that hour to plan a course of action against the new owner.

She clasped hands with Emily and they flippered their tails hard enough to swim in a circle—it was one of the trickier moves because it required a lot of core strength. Who knew mermaids needed to do a lot of sit-ups? Just as Emily let go and started to swim away, her hand got caught on the bikini strap that held up Lacy's top, tugging at the pearls and breaking the delicate strap. Lacy's breasts spilled free of the confines of the skimpy cups and she froze, completely shocked as little pearls floated downward to the bottom of the pool. For a few seconds, she didn't even think to act. Quickly she pressed her hands to her breasts and flippered hard to get to the surface of the pool, where she pulled off her goggles and the damaged top, replacing it with a spare one from her bag. God, she hoped no one had noticed.

Cam had decided to introduce himself to the folks at the bar on a Monday night, figuring the place wouldn't be too crowded. That way he could say his peace, not deal with a lot of hostility, and slip out unnoticed, never to be seen again. He'd decided to sell the place. He couldn't see running a bar or a tiki lounge or whatever you called the place, and he'd be happy with the cash. Surely these folks would understand that.

"I'll have a pint of whatever's on tap," Cameron

said as he pulled up a barstool. The tattooed lady was working again tonight. There was something particularly tough about a woman who'd gone to such lengths to tat up the length of both arms. He didn't think he could stand the pain, that's for sure.

She threw him a side-eye as she slid the beer to him. He wondered why she wasn't friendlier. That was no way to run a bar, throwing dirty looks at strangers.

He glanced over at the mermaids performing behind the glass tableau. Without Jamie distracting him—and pumping him full of drinks—he could pay more attention to the entertainment. It was pretty interesting watching the two women swim around with their tails like that. He bet it was hard to have enough power to thrust very far. When he thought of the word thrust, the first thing that came to mind these days was Lacy. Right now, he'd like nothing better than to be thrusting into her.

The redheaded mermaid was quite striking. She didn't wear goggles and her hair flowed around her as if she were an apparition. The one with the braid looked so familiar to him, but it was hard to place her in this dim light and with her eyes covered in goggles. He watched, mesmerized as the two women joined hands and flicked their tails back and forth to swim in a circle. It was erotic watching the two women shimmer and swirl underwater. The one with the braid, her body reminded him so much of Lacy it was getting him horny. Wow, if only he could get her in a mermaid's tail and a sexy top like that.

After a while, the women broke the circle, with the redhead swimming past him with a coy wave as if it was right at him. If he wasn't obsessively thinking about a naked Lacy, he'd start thinking about what it would be like to see that one minus the bikini top. He no sooner thought that than her fingers tangled in the other woman's top, breaking the strap. Her tits suddenly spilled out as she hung, suspended in the water, not doing a thing. Which gave Cam enough time to recognize who those gorgeous breasts belonged to—none other than Lacy. *Ho-ly shit.* He'd have recognized them anywhere. Hell, he'd nuzzled them with his mouth enough now that he knew every square inch of them.

Why hadn't she mentioned that she worked here? Christ, he could have been fantasizing about her as a mermaid all this time. Better yet he could have come here after hours and had her swimming naked for his eyes only. Shit. This sure as hell complicated things. Big-time.

Chapter Twenty-One

ELEVEN o'clock couldn't come soon enough for Lacy. She couldn't wait for Cameron to leave already and hoped like hell she hadn't been exposed, so to speak, and let him in on her little secret. Now that she had to admit the truth, she was embarrassed she'd kept it from him. Her lie of omission made her feel stupid and dishonest.

When the clock struck eleven, she hastened out of the pool, rinsed off, and pulled her hair into a wet, sloppy bun. Showing up at a closed bar at that hour with wet hair would be a telltale sign that you were recently swimming around like a mermaid. There was no way around this lie. She had to be honest.

She entered through the back entrance and walked over to the bar where Cam was closing out a tab with Juno.

"Cam!" she said, trying to act surprised. "What are you doing here?"

Cameron scrunched his nose. "The bigger question could be what are you doing here?"

"Wait a minute," Juno said, handing him back his credit card. She pointed at him. "You know her?" She moved her hand toward Lacy.

Edna stopped banging out her last song on the

keyboard and came over and sat down near the action. "Whoooo, Betty. This is gonna get good." She winked at Cameron.

"Uh, yeah," Cameron said. "We've been, uh, dating."

Lacy lifted her brow. Dating. So that's what they called it now. And here she thought it was an extended period of hooking up with no end date in sight.

Juno frowned. "You're dating this asshole?"

Lacy threw her a dirty look. "Okay, so I know we've spent more time in bed than actually being out in public, and perhaps we never had an actual formal date per se, but that's no reason to call him an asshole."

Edna cracked up. "Oh my God. Is this your fake date?" She pointed at Cameron, who cleared his throat and looked down at his shoes. She nodded. "He's a looker. No wonder you wanted to have sex with him."

Lacy turned five shades of red. "Edna! What are you talking about?"

"You know the conversation we had, and I told you to go for it."

She threw Edna the stink eye and quickly thrust her finger to her lips in the international sign of *shut the ever-loving fuck up*.

"Wait a minute," Juno said. "I'm so confused. You're banging the dude who's going to sell this place to developers and put us all out of a job?"

Lacy's eyes grew large. "What?"

Juno nodded at him. "That's the douchebag I overheard the other night at the bar. He got stinking drunk on Creamy Sex on the Beach drinks with some girl who encouraged him to sell this place and take the money and run, and he agreed to it."

Lacy turned to Cam. "Some girl? Would that be Jamie? Real nice girl, huh? You go get drunk with her and lie to me? Did you actually bang her before you came to my place? And what? She tells you to destroy everyone's livelihood here and get rid of this treasure that's been here since long before you were born, and you capitulated to her demands?" She pounded her fist on the bar. "And here I thought I was falling for you, but ugh, it's obvious I didn't know you at all."

Cameron made a "T" of his hands. "Whoa. Hold on everyone. Time out. I'm so damned confused. First off"—he turned to Lacy—"you're a *mermaid*? And you never thought to mention that to me?"

"I was afraid you'd think less of me." She averted his gaze. "But what about you? You own this? And you're selling it?"

"I don't even know where this information came from."

Juno aimed a thumb to her chest. "Yours truly. I was serving you drinks, and I overheard you talking about how you don't want to own this place."

"Nice that you take it upon yourself to intrude on people's conversations." He glared at her.

"Two great things about being a bartender, dude. Tips and conversation. Some of those you conduct and others you're lucky enough to hear." She grinned.

"And how does this woman know about you and me?" He nodded toward Edna.

Lacy sighed. "It's a long story."

"I seem to recall we were talking about girth."

Cameron did a double take. "You talked to her about

the size of my dick?"

Lacy shook her head vigorously. "God, no! We were talking about Billy Crapple's little dick, and then Edna sort of grabbed hold of that theme and went with it."

It was Cam's turn to shake his head. "How is it that you all seem to know what I'm doing when I don't even know? I don't even officially own the place yet, for God's sake. How could I sell it if it's not actually mine?"

"Semantics." Lacy curled her lip in disgust.

"Stop determining my intentions. I'm perfectly capable of doing that myself, thanks."

"Well, did you ever think that maybe your intentions suck? Except for sleeping with Lacy, because that was a very good decision on your part," Edna said, poofing her beehive with both hands.

"Stop already! And who are all these people?" He pointed at a small crowd that had gathered around them.

"These are the people you're putting out of work, you greedy bastard," Juno growled at him. Lacy had never heard the woman actually growl before. It made her laugh.

"Ahem." Lacy cleared her throat. "Please, allow me to introduce your staff." She extended an arm at the group of employees.

"It seems you've indirectly met Juno, our cheerful local bartender. She's fiercely loyal, and her tattoo artist girlfriend has been hard at work etching out complicated historical scenes up and down her arms for the past five years."

Cam nodded.

"Edna, well, Edna is a national treasure in these parts. She's eighty-seven-years young and as spry and sassy as the day she was born, no doubt. Edna's been playing the keyboards here since the day the place opened."

"I didn't have glasses then," she said. "And the men all loved me."

"Evidently her reputation preceded her." Lacy smiled. "Next there's Meghan, one of my fellow mermaids and a dear friend. And we've got Emily, here, who was doing a shift with me tonight—she's got the most gorgeous hair."

"Oh, then there's Stan, who comes here every night for a few hours to commiserate."

"What's he commiserating about?"

"That I have to go home to my wife."

They all laugh.

"Now, let me tell you a little something about our dear friend Vera Cosmopolous, who worked here since she was a teenager when her father started the Mermaid's Purse with the crazy idea to have a bar where people could watch mermaids swim." She took a deep breath. "Vera was taken away from us quite suddenly and we've all been in deep mourning over that loss. She was a mom, a sister, a daughter, if not literally then quite figuratively. After my mother passed, I didn't know I could feel the way I grew to do about Vera—like she was my second mother. And for Vera, whose heart was broken by a dirty rotten scoundrel, the Purse became her child that she never got to have. She tended to the place and nurtured it and all those attached to it as if it had sprung from her own loins."

Lacy looked at Cam pointedly. "And that's why Juno is so angry at the idea that you'd sell it. And to be honest, that's why we're all terribly upset about it. Not only would we lose our jobs, but our dear friendships, the legacy of this woman who's barely dead, and all for what? To put some stupid condominiums here? I know you're struggling financially, Cam, but we can come up with a better solution than to end all of this."

Chapter Twenty-Two

"LOOK, guys," he said, gazing at his rapt audience. "I mean 'guys' figuratively, being that you're mostly women. Anyhow, I'm not gonna lie. I came here tonight to wash my hands of this responsibility. I can't imagine being tied to a tiki lounge for the rest of my life. I'm an artist, not a restaurateur. I have never aspired to that level of responsibility. And to sell this, well, it would set me up for life. I could use that right about now." He heaved a big sigh.

"But I'm not an ogre. I think—I hope—Lacy can attest to that."

She blushed. He loved that she blushed because surely that meant she was thinking about how much of an ogre he wasn't in the bedroom.

"And I'd like to work with you folks to try to figure something out. Something that can help me be hands-off and earn some money and enable everyone to do their thing without a lot of hassle. Which all sounds sort of pie in the sky, doesn't it?"

Lacy shook her head. "Actually, not at all. I've been noodling on this quite a bit and have a few ideas. First off, get it designated as a national historic landmark. You can get tax deductions for doing that and it's yet another draw to the place to bring in customers."

He nodded. "Interesting idea."

"But now that I realize it's you who is taking over this place, I've got another even better idea. One I think you might like."

He stood with his arms crossed and lifted his brow. "I'm all ears."

"What about you and your painting? You lost the gallery that featured your work, but you can display your work here—maybe eventually build out a gallery adjacent to the restaurant. Not only that, but guess what? Vera lived in an awesome apartment that is part of the place. You can leave your lousy rental room and move in here."

Edna lassoed a fisted hand in the air. "You go girl," she said to Lacy, who gave her a wink.

"I gotta ask you, though, as we're all dying to know. How the hell is it that Vera left everything"—she spread her arms out—"to you?"

He shrugged. "It's the craziest thing. Somehow, we were distantly related on my mom's side. Vera met me when I was a little boy, back when my family briefly lived here. She took a fondness to me, unbeknownst to me, and way back then, she wrote me down as the sole beneficiary of the will."

Lacy shook her head. "Wow. That's incredible. It somehow seems like kismet. And I have to say it feels like Vera's reaching her hand up from the grave right now, making sure to set everything right. I think she knows you want to do the right thing by her and by us."

Cameron heaved a sigh. "I tell you what: I'd like to

sleep on this before I make any final decisions. I hope you'll all understand."

With that he turned and left them all on pins and needles, hoping he would do right by Vera.

Lacy couldn't fall asleep. She had tossed and turned for the past hour, fretting that she was somehow in the middle of this whole thing through no fault of her own. If Cam decided to bail, was everyone going to blame her? And would she blame him and be unable to let it go, thus ending their relationship?

At last, she'd started to drift off to sleep when she heard her text message buzz.

She glanced at the screen. It was from Cameron.

"Do you have a key to the restaurant?"

"Yeah. Why?"

"Don't ask. Just meet me there in ten minutes."

Okay… That had to be the strangest request she'd ever heard but sure. She quickly threw on some shorts and a T-shirt and drove to the Mermaid's Purse, where Cameron was waiting. He came around and opened her car door and enveloped her in a hug.

"I almost came knocking on your door, you know." He leaned over and pressed his forehead to hers, his eyes closed.

"So instead you dragged me from the comfort of my bed and made me come to work?"

"Well, in a sense, yes."

He pressed his lips to hers in a gentle kiss that made her heart ache.

"And by work you mean?"

"I want you to swim for me."

She looked at him as if he'd asked her to burn the place down. "Huh?"

"Please, Lacy? I'd like you to be my mermaid. I've been thinking about you ever since your top broke this evening—"

She winced. "I'd hoped no one had noticed it."

He grinned. "Are you kidding? It's how I knew it was you back there. I kept wondering why you looked so familiar. It wasn't until I saw those breasts spill out that I knew exactly who it was. It was the sexiest thing I think I've ever seen."

"So, you want me to demonstrate my mermaid skills for you at three in the morning?"

His lips curved into a sheepish grin. "Kinda sorta. But in a very specific way."

She cocked her eyebrow. "Oh? Do tell."

He grabbed her hand in his. "It was so fucking sexy watching you in there. I don't know if you noticed, but I could not take my eyes off of you the whole night. When your top fell off, well, suffice it to say that was the highlight of my week. Unfortunately I was one of too many who were privy to that show. So now, I'd like my very own private show. Starring you." He pointed at her. "Stripping naked. For me." He turned his finger to his chest.

"You're serious about this."

"Serious as a heart attack. Serious as the proprietor

of this establishment, and I need to know that you're going to be ideal mermaid material for my tiki bar."

"Omigod!" she squealed. "Does this mean you're going to keep it?"

He shrugged. "How could I not, after that sales-pitch-slash-peer-pressure session you put me through last night? I couldn't be the goat, disappointing all those people. Especially since Vera was doing me a huge favor by entrusting me with her baby. It's the only honorable thing to do, carrying the torch on her behalf."

Lacy gave him a tight hug then settled her lips over his, her tongue probing his as she explored his mouth. They kissed for a few minutes until Cameron pulled back. "Do we have a deal?"

"Let me get this straight. You want me to do a mermaid striptease for you and for you only."

He nodded. "I want to be the only man who has the privilege of watching his girlfriend get naked as a mermaid."

"Isn't that phrase 'naked as a jaybird'?"

"You, my dear, will be naked as a mermaid, however. Minus the tail." He swatted her on the butt. Now hop to it."

She gave him a wink and slipped out the back door to the pool.

She secured her clamshells over her breasts, then pulled on a dry tail from her locker. She made a mental note to figure out how to make a clear tail for next time, figuring that would be even sexier still.

She decided to not bother with her goggles. And let her hair loose so it would flow with the water. She dove into the pool and went right up to the window and waved.

Cameron grinned as he watched her. She executed some sexy twists and turns, skating her hands over her body as she did it, knowing it would make him crazy with lust. She surfaced for air, then dove deep again. This time she went up to the glass and pressed her body against it, pulling down one clamshell, then the other, and smashing her breasts against the glass. Cam stared at her, not even blinking.

She surfaced for air and tossed her top on the edge of the pool, then dove down in only her tail, swimming around. It felt super sexy with the water flowing freely over her nipples. She swam like that for several minutes, playing with her breasts as she did it. She thought about how hard Cam was watching this, and she slipped her hand down the front of her mermaid tail, playing with herself while he observed through the glass. Finally he motioned for her to remove the tail, so she pulled it down, slipping out of the flipper, letting it float to the top as she treaded water below, completely naked.

She loved that she had this audience of one, who was as turned on as she was by the mere act of performing a sensual striptease. She swam back to the top to gulp some air and grabbed her tail and flipper, placing them on the edge of the pool with her top. She'd be so embarrassed if one of the mermaids showed up tomorrow to find her clothes floating in the pool. She swam back to the window and pressed her naked body to the window. She scissored her legs so that Cam could get a good view of her pussy. Circling the pool, she did her usual mermaid twirls, minus the tail. She got lost in the sensation of the water flowing over her sensitized pussy and nipples. God, she wished Cam would be with her, and she could wrap her body around his in the water. She popped up to the surface for air again, only to see Cameron sitting on the edge of the pool, his legs dangling in the water. He reached for her and pulled her up to straddle him, dripping wet, and quickly pressed his mouth to hers as his hands roamed her body.

"Christ, Lacy, that was the sexiest thing I've ever seen in my life. Can you do that for me all the time, now that I'm the proprietor of this place?"

She smiled, unbuttoning his shorts, freeing his cock as she lifted onto her knees so she could settle down on top of his erection. "I think arrangements could be made." She raised and lowered herself over him as he pulled her breast to his mouth.

"These," he said, flicking his tongue over the nipple. "These are why I'm not selling, Lacy Caldwell. The minute I saw these gorgeous tits of yours floating freely in the water, I knew I could never sell the place." He bit down gently on one nipple while pinching the other. Their breathing intensified as she repeatedly lowered herself onto his cock, wiggling her hips as she met his thrusts. The muscles in her pelvis tightened and released like a rocket blasting into the night sky. Stars exploded behind her eyelids, and she shuddered through the remaining climax as Cameron thrust into her one final time before he came, erupting into her warmth as his cock spasmed again and again inside of her.

After a few minutes, Cam reached for the towel that Lacy had left nearby and draped it over her goose bump-covered back.

"So now that I'm going to be working alongside you," Lacy said, flashing her breasts at him, "and giving you special benefits that come with working here, how about that raise?"

They both laughed, knowing that the fringe benefits of working at the Mermaid's Purse were going to keep them there for a long, long time.

Thank you so much for reading ***Falling for Mr. No Way in Hell***! I hope you enjoyed it! If so, please help others find this book:

1. Help other people find this book by writing a review.

2. Sign up for my new releases email so you can find out about the next book as soon as it's available and get fun giveaways.
http://eepurl.com/baaewn

3. Like my Facebook page.
www.facebook.com/jennygardinerbooks

And I love to hear from readers! Let me know what you think about my books! You can write to me at jenny@jennygardiner.net, and visit me on the web at www.jennygardiner.net.

Keep reading for a sample from Falling for Mr. Sometimes, the next book in the Falling for Mr. Wrong series.

Falling

for

Mr. Sometimes

by Jenny Gardiner

Chapter One

SO maybe Jamie Lundquist had gotten a little plump, although she preferred the term "fluffy". It was a woman's prerogative, right? Especially after all of that holiday celebrating she'd just suffered through. A little Christmas party appetizers here, a little (all right, let's be honest: a *lot*) of New Year's Eve drinking there, and the next thing you know your ass is dragging, your clothes have morphed from merely snug to the oh-crap-the-zipper-of-your-jeans-won't-go-up, and you long for the days when you could pinch just an inch. Nothing a little effort at the gym (not to mention some self-restraint at mealtime) couldn't fix, right?

Which was why she found herself slogging off to Verity Beach's one and only fitness center on a frigid January morning, against her better judgment, not to mention her normal wintertime sleep patterns (uh, sleep till nine, duh). It wasn't even dawn when she arrived at the place, knowing it would be yet another day of parking space roulette. It seemed the amateurs—like her—came out by the droves to the gym in January, and parking was at an all-time premium. God forbid she park a block away and walk the extra few hundred feet; no way, man! It was freezing and she was already going to have to exert herself far more than she normally would in the dead of winter once she got inside. She had to reserve her energy stores!

So she did what she'd done every day since returning to the scene of her now-daily penance, driving sloth-slow, scouring the horizon in the hopes that someone would be pulling out and she could nab the space. She glanced to the far corner of the ample parking lot and spied what appeared to be a space, flooring it to get there before anyone else did. But once she approached, she realized that for the third time this week, some yahoo with a fancy vehicle—this time a sleek, shiny, new black SUV—had taken it upon himself (it was always a him who did this sort of thing) to straddle two spaces to protect his car from door dinks.

Dammit. This sort of thing chapped Jamie's (burgeoning) ass big-time. Didn't the moron know that January at the gym was parking lot purgatory? In the post-holiday competition to undo what the season of joy had wrought, it seemed all that good cheer was being diminished by selfish bastards like this guy, who couldn't just take a space and hope for the best with his precious car.

Well, she would show him. She sized up the remaining half-space, confident that if she couldn't fit her fat butt into her jeans, at least she could wedge her modestly-sized car into this demi-space. Thank goodness vehicles didn't gain weight with too much celebrating. She glanced in her mirror, pulled forward, then put the gear shift in reverse, checking the back-up camera on her dashboard, ever-so-gingerly drifting backward as she masterfully squeezed into the remaining void.

Jamie couldn't help but feel a bit smug about her accomplishment, even though it meant the jerk would not be able to get back into his car on the driver's side.

"That's his problem," she muttered as she put the car in park. "Let him climb in with all the spare room he has on the passenger side."

But as she checked and re-checked her positioning, she started to feel a teensy bit guilty, so she took a couple more passes to straighten up her car, even ensuring that her tires hugged the curb on the other side of the space to allow as much room as possible for Mr. Selfish to maybe—if he lost weight after his holiday binging, mind you—get into his pretentious penis-substitute-on-wheels through the driver's side door.

She turned off the ignition, exited onto the curb, and dusted off her hands, mission accomplished. She practically felt as if she'd had her exercise for the day, entertaining the idea that maybe she could even shorten her workout after this arduous park job. But no: she was here, surfing season would be upon her before she knew it, and she wasn't going to be moving up a size in a wet suit just because she took her holiday celebrating—not to mention the many stressors over her parents contentious divorce—too seriously. She was gonna wrangle that same discipline that led her to rise before dawn to surf each morning (once the weather was not so hostile) and Soul Cycle her ass down to a more manageable size.

As she fumbled in her purse for her gym pass next to the manly-man SUV, she was bowled over by the noxious fumes from what must have been a skunk or something. Yuck. The guy probably ran it over for sport. Bad enough she had to park near this jerk, but for the air

133

around her car to be enveloped in the nasty fug of skunk aroma, well, ugh. Just for good measure, she decided to slip a note onto this bonehead's windshield, letting him know—in case he was unaware—that his park job was completely lame. She rifled through her purse and pulled out a notebook and pen, pulling the cap off with her teeth. She leaned against the hood of her car as she scrawled out her message:

> *CONGRATULATIONS! YOU'VE JUST*
> *BECOME AN HONORARY MEMBER OF*
> *THE "PARK LIKE A JACKASS" CLUB.*
> *HERE'S HOPING SOME DAY YOU*
> *REDEEM YOURSELF BY LEARNING*
> *HOW TO STAY IN THE LINES.*
>
> *(p.s. your car reeks)*

She lifted one of the car's windshield wipers and secured the note beneath it, then headed into the fitness center.

After starting the day on a sour note, she was feeling good about herself, her determination, and her destiny to return to fit and petite, ASAP.

It was gonna be a great day.

Chapter Two

CARTER Henderson's day seemed to go from bad to worse. And dawn was barely breaking. This didn't bode well. First he had to jump-start the battery on his "new" used SUV, the one he'd saved up for over a year to buy. The acquisition of this vehicle was the closest he'd come to commitment in, well, ever.

Sure, he'd toughed it out through some unpleasant obligations in his life already: like living through the shitshow that had been his parents' dismal marriage the whole time he was growing up. And yeah, even though he'd realized midway through college that the accounting degree he was working toward would lead to a career that was precisely not what he wanted to do for the rest of his days on Earth, he sucked it up and graduated, despite wishing desperately that he'd gone to culinary school instead.

But now that wasn't in his meager budget, especially with paying off student loans and constantly bailing his irresponsible father out of financial jams. Instead he'd taken side jobs doing the books for a number of small businesses while working crazy hours as a sous chef at a variety of restaurants all over the Outer Banks, learning on the job how to be the best chef he could be, minus the formal training.

So even though he was tired as shit, he dragged himself out of bed in the pitch dark of a cold January morning, just to keep his commitment to himself to remember to self-care. Working his crazy hours meant if he wasn't careful, he'd end up a paunchy, sweaty, miserable, beer-bellied crank like so many chefs he'd encountered along the way. He wasn't going to be that guy.

But damn, taking care of yourself sometimes translated into kicking yourself to the curb. Certainly on days like today. Of course on his way to the gym this morning he ran over a skunk. He'd swerved to miss the thing but a few more inches and he'd have plowed into oncoming traffic, which would have made it a much worse day.

Once he got to the gym he'd vowed things would improve, pronto. Instead, he wrenched his ankle while on the treadmill, then some dumbbell actually dropped a dumbbell on his hand when he was on the ground stretching. Luckily it was a senior citizen and the weight was one of those so light you wondered why anyone even bothered to use it for resistance. He learned the hard way that it might be light, but not when it lands on a delicate body part. So yeah, this day had not gotten off to a great start.

To top it off, as he limped toward his SUV, he saw that some jerk had wedged their crap car into that space that was left after he had to straddle two spaces when he'd arrive. Annoyingly, when he'd gotten to the gym, someone next to him had overstepped the parking lines by a good two feet so he had to do the same thing. So now he wasn't going to be able to get into his damned truck, made all the worse because of his new ankle injury.

He eyeballed how the hell he was going to flatten himself like a field mouse trying to squeeze into a hole in a house. No way was he going to be able to enter through the driver's side; he'd have to be as thin as a sheet of paper to fit there. Not to mention he'd hate to dink the person's car doors, even if the guy was a jerk for parking there.

He assessed the passenger side, realizing there was no way in hell he could enter there either—the car next to him was parked in such a cockeyed way that he was stuck until the owners of those cars came out.

He cupped his hands and blew into them, failing to warm himself against the bitter cold, trying to figure out why he thought a beach town would always be warm just because it's at the beach. Totally blond mistake. Well, he was paying for that oversight now as he paced back and forth behind the SUV in his gym shorts, wishing he had coffee, or even hot water, just to warm him up—of course he hadn't brought warm-up pants along; he'd just planned to run to and from the car.

Just then he glanced over to the little Mazda two-door that had jammed in next to him and noticed the cool glow of an iPhone light in the interior the car. Well, hell—someone must've been in there all along. He raced over to the driver's side door and pounded on the window.

He saw a pretty face turn and stare at him, but she didn't put the window down. He banged on the window again, steam billowing from his nose from the cold temperatures.

Finally she lowered window about a millimeter. She must've been one of those women—the kind who think every guy is out to hurt you. Sheesh, he'd had enough of paranoid chicks like that. The last gal he'd dated came out and told him it was only a matter of time before he hurt her, either physically or emotionally, because that's what guys do. *What the fuck?* Alas, she was sort of prescient with that comment, because he immediately broke it off with her. Who wanted to be with a kook like that?

He put his face close to the crack in the window and spoke.

"Look, could you move you car? You've kind of parked me in." He pointed toward the SUV, which was almost like the Siamese twin to her car, they were so close together.

He could see through the window that she was furrowing her brows.

"Yeah, I'll move it," she said, pausing. "But next time could you please be consider of others and only take up one parking space?"

Carter stopped in his tracks. Suddenly he no longer felt cold, but instead the heat of unrepentant fury ignite in his body like a fireball bursting through the atmosphere.

"Excuse me?" he said, his voice raising an octave. He knocked on the window as if he needed to get closer access to her to be sure she actually had the gonads to say that to him. His mind felt like one of those metal balls in a pinball machine that pings from place to place in a random yet violent way each time it hits a bumper that powers it elsewhere within its limited confines.

She cracked her window just a tiny bit more. "I said: please, next time just use one space."

He thought his head might erupt like one of those volcanoes where the top of the thing blasts right off of it from pent-up activity within its core.

"Are you fucking kidding me?" he said, his pulse escalating as if he'd just gotten it up to one seventy on the treadmill again. "You're telling *me* how to fucking park?"

She frowned. "Judging by how you did this time, it appears you need the assistance."

He waggled a finger at her vehicle. "Says you, who shoved your car so far up my car's ass it's gonna have to crap it out."

"You left me no choice. I'm sick and tired of inconsiderate—"

"Inconsiderate? *Inconsiderate?*" he paused, fixing his gaze on her as the first barbs of sunlight illuminated this, this, this Judge Judy bitch sitting there making determinations about which she knew absolutely nothing. "Listen, sweetheart." He pressed his finger right up on the window at her. "Clearly you've been packing on the pounds, dough girl. Maybe you should be spending more time in there," he extended his arm toward the gym, his hand trembling with fury, "And less time out here picking fights with complete strangers."

Suddenly the woman rolled her window down the rest of the way. This was perfect. He was gonna give her a piece of his mind and tell her where she could shove her arrogant presumptions. But before he got even a half a syllable out of his mouth, she reached her arm out and chucked her cup of coffee all over his ski jacket and gym shorts. Then she put the car in drive and pulled out before he even had a chance to retaliate. Not that he would have. But still.

And he heard her exclaim, as she drove out of sight, "I'd rather be fat on the outside than ugly on the inside like you!" Which caused his soul to shrivel just a bit, because he actually couldn't blame her for saying.

Granted, he'd been shivering from the cold a few minutes ago, but this was not the way he'd hoped to heat up, with a cup of relatively hot coffee tossed all over him. Damned woman. This was precisely why he didn't deal with women to begin with: they were all irrational, hot–headed and mean-spirited.

He took a few deep breaths, trying to calm himself down, unlocked the door to his SUV with the key fob, and hopped into the driver's seat. As he stuck the key into the ignition, he saw her note on the other side of his windshield, staring at him across the dashboard as he scanned her little nastygram.

Damned woman—got the last word on him twice. Well, that will be the last time he let's some Type A jerk like her get under his skin. He'd see to that.

Falling for Mr. Sometimes
Coming May 15, 2018

About the Author

Jenny Gardiner is the author of #1 Kindle Bestseller *Slim to None* and the award-winning novel *Sleeping with Ward Cleaver*. Her latest works are the *It's Reigning Men* series, the *Royal Romeos* series and her new *Falling for Mr. Wrong* series. She also published the memoir *Winging It: A Memoir of Caring for a Vengeful Parrot Who's Determined to Kill Me,* now re-titled *Bite Me: a Parrot, a Family and a Whole Lot of Flesh Wounds*; the novels *Anywhere but Here*; *Where the Heart Is*; the essay collection *Naked Man on Main Street*, and *Accidentally on Purpose* and *Compromising Positions* (writing as Erin Delany); and is a contributor to the humorous dog anthology *I'm Not the Biggest Bitch in This Relationship*.

Her work has been found in Ladies Home Journal, the Washington Post, Marie-Claire.com, and on NPR's Day to Day. She was also a columnist for Charlottesville's Daily Progress for over a decade, and is the Volunteer Coordinator for the Virginia Film Festival.

She has worked as a professional photographer, an orthodontic assistant (learning quite readily that she was not cut out for a career in polyester), a waitress (probably her highest-paying job), a TV reporter, a pre-obituary writer, as well as a publicist to a United States Senator (where she first learned to write fiction). She's photographed Prince Charles (and her assistant husband got him to chuckle!), Elizabeth Taylor, and the president of Uganda. She and her family and menagerie of pets now live a less exotic life in Virginia.

Visit Jenny at her website at www.jennygardiner.net where you can sign up for her newsletter, visit her blog, or find her on Facebook and Twitter. And every blue moon she'll post adorable pictures of her pets on Instagram as @thejennygardiner.